JINGLE ALL THE WAY TO SNOWSIDE

A SWEET CHRISTMAS ROMANCE

A VERMONT CHRISTMAS ROMANCE—THE
MURPHY CLAN

BOOK TWO

KATHY COATNEY

Windtree
Press

GET A FREE BOOK

Angels R' Us

Saving lost souls is hard work. Just ask Olivia and Zack, two angels who've been assigned to bring Maggie and Ian together. Zack was Olivia's CIA partner in life, and he's become her nemesis in death. What Olivia doesn't realize is that Zack has vowed to love her into eternity.

Subscribe to my newsletter to get your copy of Angels R' Us here.
https://kathycoatney.com/subscribe

COPYRIGHT

ACKNOWLEDGMENTS

I've had a number of life-altering moments in my life, each special in their own way. The road to becoming a novelist has been smooth and rocky, but it has been an incredible journey because of those who have accompanied me.

My faithful email check-in pal, Jennifer Skullestad; my critique partner, Luann Erickson; my beta readers, Wendy Delaney, Rebecca Clark, and Jody Burnchinal Sherin—you guys are my GPS to finding the end. My writing pals, Karen Duvall and Marie Harte. Friends and family made the journey memorable —Karol Black, Diana McCollum, Tammy Lambeth, and my family—Nick, Wade and Devin, Collin and Ellis, Jake and Emily, Allie and Russell. I'm blessed to have had you all beside me.

I've also had the pleasure to work with several talented businesswomen: Laura Shin, my editor, and Tara with Fantasia Frog Design, my cover designer.

DEDICATION

To my dear friend Jody Burchinal Sherin. I felt you guiding me with every word I wrote.

ALSO BY KATHY COATNEY

Thank you for reading *Jingle all the Way to Snowside,* book two in *A Vermont Christmas Romance—The Murphy Clan series*.

If you liked this book, I'd love it if you'd leave a review at Goodreads and BookBub.

I love hearing from my fans. You can contact me through my website, newsletter, or join my Facebook group Kathy Coatney's The Beauty Bowl. I share information about my books, excerpts, and other fun information. If you like free books come join Kathy Coatney's Review Team by sending me an email kathy@kathycoatney.com.

All my books are small town, contemporary romances with uplifting stories of hope, a sprinkling of quirky characters and a happily ever after sure to leave you with a smile.

Contact me at:

Website

Kathy Coatney's The Beauty Bowl

The Murphy Clan

Falling in Love series

Falling For You...Again

Falling in Love With You

Falling in Love For The First Time

Falling in Love With Him

Return to Hope's Crossing series

Forever His

Forever Mine

Forever Yours

Crooked Halo Christmas Chronicles

Be My Santa Tonight

Her Christmas Wish

Under the Mistletoe

The Christmas Kiss—A Sweet Christmas Romance

A Vermont Christmas Romance

Santa Comes to Snowside

Jingle all the Way to Snowside

Box Sets

Falling in Love Box Set

Return to Hope's Crossing Box Set

The Murphy Clan Mixed Collection

Crooked Halo Christmas Chronicles Box Set

JINGLE ALL THE WAY TO SNOWSIDE

Sweet Christmas romance. Check. Matchmaking Santa and Mrs. Claus. Check, check. Two lonely hearts. Check, check, check!

She's a country girl living in the heart of the city. He's an ex-SEAL teaching kindergarteners.

Sadie McCluskey loved the holidays until she lost her parents in a car accident at sixteen, then her ex-husband left her a week before Christmas. She's content spending the holidays working her urban farm until Hank Dabrowski walks into her life. Now, all she wants is to get Hank under the mistletoe.

Hank needed a change after ten years as a SEAL. When he breaks off his engagement, he leaves his hometown of Angel Falls, Vermont, and moves to Snowside to teach kindergarteners! Burned, but not broken, Hank still believes in true love, especially after Sadie gives his kids a tour of her farm. Watching her share her joy of farming with them ignites a spark deep inside him. But can he convince her he's the Christmas gift she's been longing for?

Jody and Nick Claws arrive on Sadie's doorstep in matching red and green plaid flannel shirts, the spitting image of that other jolly yuletide couple. Can these holiday matchmakers work their Christmas magic to help two reluctant hearts find their happily ever after?

Nothing kicks off the holidays like a pair of lonely hearts in need of Christmas magic, so grab your copy today.

PROLOGUE

Somewhere north of Vermont

Nick Claws finished polishing the hood of the candy red Mini Cooper and began loading it with suitcases. By the time he'd finished, there was only room for him, Jody, and their miniature poodle, Prancer. His wife had never learned the art of packing light.

The October sun crept over the horizon. Fingers of sunlight cascaded over the trunk as Nick wedged the last suitcase into the trunk.

"So why are we headed to Snowside in October?" Jody asked, coming up to him with Prancer snuggled in her arms. The miniature poodle lifted his head and gave a single bark, as if he also wanted an answer to the question.

Nick glanced over at her, his blue eyes twinkling as he stroked his long, white beard. "We're getting an early start on the Christmas season."

"The earliest we've ever gone is November."

"You're right, but this one's going to be a bit more challenging, and we're going to need more time since we'll be volunteering at two different sites."

Jody looked down at Prancer. "Did you hear that?" she asked the dog. "We're starting Christmas in October this year."

"Is that a bad thing?" Nick asked.

"Absolutely not. You know I love Christmas. I can't think of anything better than starting now." Jody clapped her hands, excitement pulsing through her. "So, tell me where we'll be volunteering."

He helped her into the car, and they set off. "As you know, we're returning to Snowside, and there's the sweetest woman, Sadie McCluskey. She runs McCluskey River Farm right in downtown Snowside. It's only three acres, but it's got all the charm of the Old Time Christmas Tree Farm and Enchanted Inn that Jeremy and Marilyn Clark own. It's the place we gave Jack and Annie Bradshaw the sleigh ride and romantic dinner almost four years ago. Sadie grows every crop imaginable and does all kinds of weekly events, from brunches to movie nights, crafts for kids and adults, tours of the farm, and she teaches classes on growing successful gardens. But she desperately needs help with the events, which is where you come in. I know you're going to love it!"

"I can't wait to get started. And what about the other place?"

"It's a kindergarten classroom, and the teacher is Hank Dabrowski. His hands are full, and he really needs more help in the classroom. He's dedicated to these kids and their families and wants to do more than just teach them. Many of his kids' families are living hand-to-mouth, so he's determined to not only educate the kids, but improve their lives."

Jody faced him, her reindeer earrings swaying against rosy cheeks. "So, I assume there's a connection between Sadie and Hank?"

Nick cast a side-long glance at his wife, then focused on the road. "Yes. The land Sadie farms is owned by our old friend Elroy Murphy—one of our first holiday matchups and Hank's great-uncle. Elroy actually wrote to us about them. From what he said, he promised Sadie that he will never allow the land to be anything but farmland, and he's waiting for her to come up with the financing to buy it. She's applied for numerous loans, but keeps getting turned down. Hank's been trying to convince his uncle to contact a lawyer to ensure he gets fair market value for the land, which could mean Sadie would lose her farm."

Jody clapped her hands over her mouth, shaking her head. "We can't have Sadie lose that farm. It's too important. We're going to have to convince Hank to change his mind."

Nick nodded in agreement.

"Are Hank and Sadie our holiday matchup?"

"They are, but it's going to be a challenge. Hank is driven to make a difference for his students, but he's suspicious of Sadie, especially after a bad breakup. Sadie is committed to her farm, but her resistance goes deeper. Her parents died when she was in high school, and she went into foster care. Then she married young and her ex-husband hurt her deeply. Now, she's afraid to love and she's lost her Christmas spirit."

Jody tapped a finger to her lips as she thought over the problem. "Well, we're going to have our work cut out for us, but we will find a solution."

Nick reached over and squeezed her knee. "That's what I love most about you—your optimism. You don't believe in can't."

Jody winked at him, tracing her fingers over his cheek as she stared into his face. "I couldn't do it without you."

Nick punched the gas. Jody's laughter floated on the air again as they jetted down the highway.

CHAPTER 1

S adie lifted the brim of her straw hat and swiped at the perspiration gathered on her forehead. Shading her eyes, she stared up at the cloudless blue sky. She couldn't remember an October this warm.

She finished clearing the last raised-bed planter and sat back on her haunches, studying the freshly tilled soil, rich and dark as Columbian coffee. The same sense of satisfaction filled her at the end of every season. Ready for a break, but eagerly awaiting spring planting. Nothing gave her more pleasure than watching new crops burst from the ground. They temporarily filled the void for the children she yearned for, but didn't have.

An ache stabbed through her at the things missing from her life, but she quickly shoved it aside when she heard, "Aunt Sadie."

She turned and saw Zoe racing toward her from the circa-1895 farmhouse. The land came with two houses on either end of the three-acre property. The old farmhouse nearest downtown Snowside she'd converted into a deli with an upstairs office. The other farmhouse, near the river and further away from the traffic and hustle and bustle of the city, she lived in.

She rose and swooped the three-year-old into her arms, swinging her high in the air, then spinning in a circle. Not her niece by blood, but she and Zoe's mother, Annie Bradshaw Davidson, were as close as sisters.

Giggles erupted.

She pulled her close, squeezing her tight. Zoe planted a slobbery kiss on Sadie's cheek that was as gooey as the ones Sweet Pea, Sadie's two-year-old Bernese Mountain Dog, gave her first thing every morning.

The canine, who'd been chasing grasshoppers, bounded over when she saw Zoe. The little girl squealed with delight and wiggled out of Sadie's arms to hug Sweet Pea.

"What are you doing here?" Sadie asked Zoe as she wiped the juicy kiss from her cheek.

Zoe pointed a chubby finger behind her where Jack, Annie's husband, came toward her, then buried her face in Sweet Pea's tricolored fur. The dog released a satisfied sigh. She loved everyone, but Zoe most of all.

Sadie turned to Jack and gave him a one-armed hug. "I thought you were working today."

"We have a surprise for you," Zoe said.

Jack pressed a finger to his lips. "Wait till Mom gets here."

Sadie arched a brow as Zoe slapped a hand over her mouth to prevent the giggles from escaping and failing.

A moment later, Annie made her way over to them, her face sallow.

Zoe released Sweet Pea and raced over to her mother, grabbing her hand and tugging her forward. "Hurry up, Mama. We have to tell Aunt Sadie our surprise."

Annie swallowed, but allowed her daughter to drag her over.

Zoe jumped up and down, and Sweet Pea got into the excitement, dancing and barking. "Tell her, tell her, tell her!"

Jack and Annie exchanged a look with the little girl. "Why don't you show her?"

A grin almost as wide as Sweet Pea's massive chest filled her face. She took the picture her mother held out and shoved it at Sadie. "I'm going to have a baby sister!"

Sadie stared at the sonogram, then at Annie and Jack, her heart overflowing with love for the woman who was the closest thing to family she had. She and Annie had met when Sadie rode the downtown bus Annie drove. In fact, Sadie had even been there when Zoe was born, which had cemented their friendship. Two weeks away from the due date and still driving, Annie's water had broken. Twenty minutes later, Zoe arrived ahead of the EMTs. Fortunately, Jack made it in the nick of time to catch his daughter.

"You're going to be an aunt again," Zoe announced with all the pride of the banty rooster that ruled Sadie's henhouse.

Sadie swooped Zoe into her arms again, and they danced in a circle. "I can't wait."

Jack and Annie stood beside them, watching their antics. "We don't know that the baby is a girl, Zoe," Jack reminded his daughter.

A petulant expression came over Zoe's face as Sadie set her on the ground. "I do, and I'm telling Santa I want a sister, *not* a brother."

Sadie grinned. "I don't care if it's a girl or boy. I just think it's wonderful you guys are having another baby." She looked down at Zoe. "What do you say we celebrate with apple cider and cookies?"

Zoe clapped her hands. "Do you have the monster cookies?"

Her question drew laughter from the adults. Zoe called Sadie's homemade granola bars monster cookies. "Of course."

Zoe skipped across the dirt path with Sweet Pea on her heels as the adults followed them back to the old farmhouse.

"So how goes it at Job Hunters 4 You?" Sadie asked. The nonprofit that Jack and his uncle, Mickey, ran helped people find jobs by providing clothing, showers, haircuts, and assistance with résumés and interviews.

"Amazing," Annie gushed. "You've got to come by and check it out for yourself. Jack added two more chairs in the salon. They've also expanded their clothing and shoe section, and now the showers are open."

"You've convinced me. I'll be by this weekend." She changed the subject. "Are you still driving the short route?" she asked Annie.

Annie nodded. She'd gone from full-time to a part-time route after Zoe was born. She and Jack worked their schedules so that Zoe could be with Jack while she drove. And some days, Jack and Zoe rode with her.

They passed the barn adjacent to the deli where they held brunches and movie nights when Sadie could find time to squeeze them in. They kept growing in popularity, so much so, she needed an event planner to keep up with it.

Climbing the porch steps, they went inside the gift shop/deli/coffee house with tables and chairs to sip coffee, enjoy a mid-day meal, or dessert. Someday Sadie hoped to convert it into a full-scale restaurant using food from the farm—if she could ever get a loan to buy the land and do all the improvements on her wish list, which continued to grow.

Jack and Annie found a table while Sadie got juice and cookies for Zoe. Glancing over at them, a bittersweet wave of envy swept over her. Once upon a time, she'd hoped she and Luke, her ex, would have the love and happiness her friend had found.

Sadie shook off the melancholy. She and Luke were over. He'd moved on, married, and had the family Sadie had always dreamed of. Time she faced reality—marriage and children weren't in the cards for her.

SADIE WENT UPSTAIRS to her office after Annie and Jack left, Sweet Pea trailing after her. Sweet Pea flopped on her bed next to the desk as Sadie sat down at the computer.

She logged on and sucked in a breath when an email popped up from the agriculture department.

Third times a charm.

She sure hoped so because she didn't know what she'd do if they rejected her application this time. Elroy Murphy, her landlord, friend, and mentor and a distant cousin of Annie's, had urged her to apply for funding through a federal program to buy the land. Hordes of real estate developers were eager to scoop up the prized piece of property and turn it into high-rise condos for the wealthy or, God forbid, another skyscraper. Elroy received daily pressure to sell, but he'd flat-out refused. This land would remain farmland, and he'd even changed his will to reflect his wishes. Everything had been fine until his great-nephew moved to Snowside.

Hank Dabrowski.

The man had out-and-out accused her of taking advantage of Elroy. What nerve!

Sadie paid her rent on time, took excellent care of the property, and Elroy had been the one to suggest she buy it, not the other way around. But that didn't stop *Godzilla*, as she thought of the hulking ex-SEAL, from insinuating she'd tricked his uncle into selling her the farm at below market price.

A fat lot he knew. Elroy might have offered it to her at a ridiculously low price—and even offered to carry the note—but she'd told him that she would pay full price for it and refused to consider his offer to carry the note. She wouldn't tie up his money.

Godzilla had tried intimidation. While that might have worked in the military, it didn't fly with her. She couldn't deny the man was insanely attractive with those chiseled cheekbones, square jaw, and shoulders so broad he almost had to turn sideways to fit through the door.

Looks weren't everything, and his accusations killed any flicker of desire she might have carried.

Really?

She pushed the annoying voice aside and opened her email, then swore.

Dear Ms. McCluskey:

We regret to inform you we must reject your application. The land is zoned residential. We only approve loans with agricultural zoning...

Sadie rolled her chair away from the computer without reading the rest.

Standard rejection.

Pacing the length of the office, she searched for a solution. The city had refused her request for rezoning. The banks wouldn't touch her. Too risky, they'd said, even though she'd been profitable for years. The agriculture department had been her last shot.

She closed her eyes, pressing her forehead to the window, despair making her chest hurt. A low whine and a wet nose nudged her hand, forcing her eyes open. Squatting beside Sweet Pea, she hugged her.

"It's okay, girl. I'll figure something out. Don't worry."

Dark eyes flecked with copper stared back at her.

Sadie stroked the glossy black fur, silently promising she wouldn't let her down. She loved this place and wasn't giving up. Somehow she would find a way to buy this land.

CHAPTER 2

Hank Dabrowski parked his late-model F-150 beside the McCluskey River Farm sign and stared out the windshield.

The last thing he wanted was another standoff with Sadie McCluskey, but he'd promised Elroy he'd apologize.

His shoulders bunched as he recalled his last meeting with Sadie that had ended in a shouting match. Not his finest hour.

He dealt with rambunctious kindergarteners all day, but he'd gone ballistic with the green-eyed spitfire with tawny-brown locks. What had gotten into him?

A mix of fear and desire, that's what. He wouldn't be deceived again by a pretty face. Pretty ha! Try stunning.

He pushed thoughts of Sadie aside, picked up the flowers from the passenger seat, and headed inside. Climbing the wide porch steps, he pushed open the door to the Old Farmhouse Deli.

An electronic bell chimed when he entered, a neon sign flashing closed sat on the deli counter.

Good, he could grovel in private.

"Hello," he called out.

A bark, followed by the clatter of nails against hardwood,

announced Sweet Pea's arrival. Skidding to a halt beside him, she danced circles around him.

He leaned down to scratch Sweet Pea's ears as Sadie's voice echoed from the stairwell, "We're closed."

A vision of the green-eyed beauty with the impossibly thick lashes and a body that kept him awake at night sent inappropriate thoughts charging through him that he quickly squelched.

Not going there. He'd come to grovel, not ogle.

"The sign says open," he called back.

Sadie appeared, a welcoming smile on her face, until she spotted him. "We're closed," she repeated, mistrust evident in her tone.

Not that he blamed her after their last meeting. "I know it's late, but could you spare a few minutes?"

Sadie's arms folded over her chest. "So you can accuse me of taking advantage of Elroy again?"

Sweet Pea plopped on the floor between them, her dark gaze fixed on her master.

"No. I was out of line, and I'm sorry." He held out the bouquet. "I shouldn't have said the things I did."

She held her ground. "No, you shouldn't have." Her gaze softened as she traced a finger over the flowers. "I do love lilies," she murmured.

Her cheeks turned a fetching pink Hank found appealing. Hell, truth be told, he found her incredibly attractive.

She took the bouquet, leaned forward, and inhaled. "They smell amazing. Thank you."

"You're welcome."

"You didn't have to do this." She smiled shyly at him, and a stab of desire shot through him again.

Where the hell had that come from? He'd come here to reason with her, not ask her out.

12

Taking a breath, he said, "Do you have a minute to discuss the deal between you and Uncle Elroy?"

She bristled. "I thought you came to apologize."

"I did."

"Doesn't feel that way to me." She thrust the flowers into his hands.

Sweet Pea whined, pleading with him to fix it.

"It's time for you to leave. Any conversation about the sale of property you need to have with Elroy."

"I've tried, but he won't discuss it with me."

"Your problem, not mine." She pulled open the door, glaring at him. "It's been a long day."

Hank stepped outside and before he could comment further, she slammed the door in his face.

Sweet Pea pressed her nose to the window, staring out at him, her dark eyes solemn and silently berated him.

You really botched that, Dabrowski.

With a frustrated sigh, he climbed into his truck, tossed the flowers on the seat and drove off.

"I SEE WHAT YOU MEAN," Jody said, watching as Sadie locked the store, and she and Sweet Pea headed down the path to her house.

"They are both overreacting," Nick said.

Jody gave a soft grunt in agreement. "They are, but I don't think it's all about selling the land. Did you feel the energy zipping between them like elves building Christmas toys?"

"I did. Are you thinking that's the source of their animosity?"

"I am, and I'm thinking Sweet Pea will play a role in bringing them together."

"How so?"

Jody stroked Prancer. "Dogs are much smarter than people

give them credit for. Did you see how she reacted to their argument?" A rhetorical question, and she didn't give Nick an opportunity to respond. "She sees those two are meant to be together."

"What's our next move?"

Jody grinned. "We roll up our sleeves and get to work."

CHAPTER 3

"Who knows what letter this is?" Hank held up a block with the letter A printed on it, calling out to his group of boisterous five-year-olds.

Two hands immediately shot up, waving wildly like a thrill ride at the carnival—the same two who always responded. Henry bounced in his seat, impatient to answer as Kirstin elbowed him back to be sure Hank didn't miss her hand flapping in the air.

Nobody missed Kirstin. Sweet as apple pie and a heart as big as the enormous red gummy bear at Sweetheart Candies, she always made sure all her classmates felt included.

Barbie, the little girl next to Kirstin, really needed to be drawn out of her shell. Barbie did everything possible to avoid being called on or to bring attention to herself.

Hank desperately wanted to change that, and apparently Kirstin sensed his intent because she dropped her hand and placed it on Barbie's shoulder, whispering gentle encouragement into her ear.

Her thoughtfulness touched Hank deeply.

When Barbie didn't respond, Hank called on the still bouncing Henry. Labeled hyperactive, but Hank wasn't convinced. Henry needed movement to temper his energy, and once he had it, he'd become an exceptional student.

The bell rang. Hank and his aide, Rosario, led the children outside for recess.

He'd been pressuring the administration for another aide, but so far, his requests had fallen on deaf ears. Even attending the school board meetings hadn't generated more help, but Hank wasn't giving up. He'd do anything for his kids.

THE LAST BELL RANG, and parents came to collect their children.

Cyrus Blackstone's father arrived ten minutes late to a clearly distressed child. His dad squatted down to his level and took his hands. "Sorry I'm late. I couldn't leave work."

A frequent occurrence, but Darious Blackstone worked two jobs to support his family after his wife had left a year ago and moved to California. Alone, Darious cared for his three children, living paycheck-to-paycheck.

Cyrus's lip trembled. "I was afraid you left like Mama did."

Darious drew the little boy into his arms. "I will never leave you." He squeezed him to his chest, then pulled back to look him in the eye. "I promise. Okay?"

Cyrus sniffled and nodded.

"Okay, let's get your brothers and go home."

Cyrus grabbed his backpack, a tremulous smile lifting his lips as he swiped the tears from his cheeks. "See you tomorrow, Mr. D."

Dabrowski was a mouthful for his five-year-olds, so he'd shortened it to Mr. D.

Hank waved goodbye and wished, not for the first time, he could do more to help his students and their families.

HANK FINISHED CLEANING the classroom and was about to head home when a tap sounded on the door. He looked up and there stood what he could only describe as Santa and Mrs. Claus dressed in red pants and green and red plaid tops.

"Can I help you?" he asked.

The woman grinned, a smattering of spiderweb wrinkles creasing blue eyes that spoke of a life filled with joy and happiness. "I'm Jody and this is my husband, Nicky Claws."

His face must've given away his skepticism because she burst into giggles.

"That's Claws spelled *C-L-A-W-S*."

Hank immediately liked the two. "What can I do for you?" he asked as he ushered them inside.

Nick's jolly laughter echoed through the classroom. "It's more what we can do for you."

Hank stared at the two in confusion. "How so?"

Jody squeezed her husband's hand. "Nicky would like to volunteer in your classroom."

Hank stared at them, dumbfounded by the offer. "You understand my kids are five-year-olds, right?"

Jody gave him a vigorous nod. "Of course."

A few parents volunteered occasionally, but most worked. Nick's age, however, concerned him. Would he be able to keep up with the children? Of course, he could find things for him to do that didn't require the constant running he and Rosario did.

"How did you hear about my classroom?"

Jody's eyes twinkled with what Hank could only describe as delight. "Nicky and I take on a holiday project every year, and when Elroy sent us a letter telling us about your class, Nick wanted to help kiddos get the best start in school. Your classroom seemed like the perfect fit."

Elroy had written to them about his class? "How do you know my uncle?"

Jody's smile widened. "Elroy's wife, your aunt, Myra, was a distant cousin of mine." She turned to her husband. "Do you still have the letter?"

Nick reached into the red bag at his feet that looked an awful lot like Santa's bag and pulled out an envelope, handing it to Hank.

Hank opened the letter and skimmed the contents.

My nephew teaches kindergarteners here in Snowside. His students love him, but he needs help. I've listened to him speak at the school board meetings, asking the district to provide funding for more teacher's aides, but so far they've done nothing. Please help him.

Elroy.

Hank carefully folded the paper, slipping it back in the envelope, then returned it to Nick, shaking his head and smiling. Elroy always had his back. "When did he send this?"

Nick shrugged, looking at Jody. "I'm not sure. A few weeks ago, don't you think?"

Jody nodded, her elf earrings bobbing.

Hank had started teaching here last winter when he'd taken over for the previous teacher who was on maternity leave. He'd needed a fresh start after his breakup with Lydia, so when Elroy mentioned the opening at Snowside Elementary, he'd applied. How his uncle had heard about the position, Hank didn't have a clue, but they'd hired him to finish the school year. At the end of the term, a permanent position became available, and he'd accepted it.

He looked at Jody, who watched him expectantly.

"Can you use our help?" she asked.

Words failed him. Finally, he pulled himself together and said, "How can I turn down such a generous offer?"

Jody clapped her hands and grinned, startling a bark from the dog in her bag. "Wonderful. Nicky will be here first thing in the morning."

Hank nodded, still shell-shocked. He had help. He could do so much more with another pair of hands in the classroom. "Thank you."

Nick and Jody rose. She hugged Hank, and Nick shook his hand. "I'll be here bright and early," Nick promised.

Within moments they were gone, leaving Hank to wonder if they'd been real, or a figment of his imagination.

CHAPTER 4

The bell chimed as Sadie finished up her day after sending Dale, her deli manager, home.

Sweet Pea barked and wagged her tail, rushing over to the door before Sadie could grab her collar.

She looked up, an apologetic smile in place as she was about to explain they were closed, when the words froze her throat. A couple stood in her doorway, a tiny dog in the woman's arms dressed in a Christmas sweater and a pair of antlers that Sweet Pea sniffed with avid interest.

"I'm sorry, we're closed," Sadie stuttered.

The woman waved off her comment, her eyes twinkling like the lights Sadie hung above the tables at Sunday brunch on the farm.

"We're not here to buy anything," she said. "I'm Jody and this is my husband, Nick Claws—*C-L-A-W-S*. We're here to offer our services."

Sadie gazed at her in confusion. "Services?"

The woman's smile warmed Sadie's heart.

Intrigued, Sadie said, "I was about to watch the sunset with a cup of coffee. Would you care to join me?"

"We'd be delighted," Jody said.

Sadie poured three coffees, then led them out to the all-season porch. Sweet Pea laid down at Nick's feet and Prancer curled up next to her, promptly falling asleep.

"Do you live in Snowside?" Sadie asked.

"Oh, my, no. We live far north of here. We come down for the holidays, but we came a little early this year."

"Do you have family in Snowside?" Sadie asked.

Hearty laughter bubbled from Nick, echoing over the tiny space and muting out the continual hum of the traffic. "We have family all over the world. We were here a few years ago and helped some friends of yours—Jack and Annie Davidson."

Sadie's eyes went wide, and she nearly choked on her coffee when they mentioned Annie and Jack. She'd heard all about these two, but she'd been so busy over the holidays that year, she'd never gotten an opportunity to meet them. "You were the match-makers, right?"

A cunning glimmer entered Jody's eyes. "We couldn't take credit for that. Let's just say we enabled the circumstances that brought them together."

Sadie didn't miss the conspiratorial glance between the two. "So, what brings you here?"

Nick deferred to Jody. "You tell her."

"A little birdie told us you need an event planner, and I'm here to offer my services," Jody said.

Sadie's mouth dropped before she quickly snapped it closed. "How did you hear about that?" When they didn't respond, she said, "Okay, it's true I need help. My events are expanding so rapidly I can't keep up. Do you know anything about event planning?"

The gleam of Nick's pearly whites lit up the oncoming dark-ness. "Jody is the queen of event planning, and she does it all year long." He turned to his wife. "Isn't that right?"

She nodded.

Prancer cracked open an eye and gave a muffled bark of agreement.

"What are your fees?"

Nick's brows drew together. "Fees? We don't charge. We volunteer."

"Oh, I couldn't ask you to do that," Sadie objected. "I'm looking to hire someone."

"Until you do, I'm here to fill in," Jody said. "And you'll have time to hire someone who will be a perfect fit, rather than take the first applicant that comes along."

It would definitely ease the pressure to find an event coordinator. Sadie studied the pair, and it was downright serendipitous how these two showed up at the perfect time to give her the ability to wait and hire the very best person for the job. "How can I say no?"

"You can't, and I'll be here bright and early tomorrow morning."

Sadie glanced between the two. Suddenly, the tightness between her shoulders eased. Maybe she didn't have to carry the burden of the farm all on her own.

HANK ARRIVED at Jobs Hunters 4 You just before closing that evening. He found Mickey at the front desk, his bald head shining in the glow of the overhead lights. His old pal came around and pounded his back. Tall and brawny like most of his SEAL team.

He and Mickey had lost contact until Mickey's nephew, Jack Davidson, opened the nonprofit.

"Where the hell have you been?" Mickey asked, beaming at him.

That was the thing Hank loved most about Mickey, the ready

smile and boisterous laughter, although for the life of him, he'd never envisioned Mickey as a hairdresser. Of course, who would've thought he'd end up teaching kindergartners?

Go figure, right?

"Sorry, it's been a busy week. I sent one of my parents over here. Do you know if they showed up?"

"Conner Miller. Is that who you're talking about?"

"Yes, that's him. Were you able to help him?"

"We were. I gave him a cut and shave, and Jack got him a suit and interview. I heard they offered him the job."

Hanks shoulders sagged. "That's a relief." At least that had worked out. Too bad his apology to Sadie hadn't gone as well.

Mickey studied him. "I get the feeling that's not the only thing on your mind."

Before Hank could respond, Mickey nodded toward the back. "Let's grab a beer and talk on the roof."

Mickey lived above Job Hunters 4 You in the second-floor industrial apartment. A nice place, but Hank envied the rooftop patio with views of the river and the city.

Ready for some kickback time after the week he'd put in, Hank followed his friend upstairs.

Settling into the deck chairs, they watched the sun tilt low in the sky reflecting off the glass buildings in the business district as the evening chill settled over them.

"How goes school?" Mickey asked.

Hank took a long pull of his beer and leaned back in the chair, the stress of the day slipping away. "All in all, good. There are always problems, of course, but nothing like our time in the Middle East."

Mickey clinked his bottle to Hank's. "Definitely."

"How about you?" Hank asked.

Mickey smiled, his eyes crinkling in the corners. "Doing well. The hair salon downtown is crazy busy, but ever since the remodel that added two more chairs, the number of clients I have here has tripled. The word is out, and Jack has to hire more staff."

"That's good news, right?"

"Absolutely, especially with the grants he's received. He wants to expand further by providing temporary housing."

Hank's pulse accelerated. "That would be amazing. Keep me posted on that, would you? I've been attending city council meetings trying to get them to address this issue."

"I will." He took a sip of his beer, then fixed his gaze on Hank. "So, what's bothering you?"

Hank shifted in his chair. Mickey could always read him. "I tried to apologize to Sadie McCluskey."

Mickey's gaze didn't waver. "I'm assuming by *try* it blew up in your face?"

Hank winced. "You could say that."

His friend shook his head. "What did you do?"

Why did Mickey assume it was his fault?

Because it was, dumbass.

Hank told his friend about the botched apology and tamped down his annoyance with Mickey's continual eye rolls. By the time he finished, the sun had dipped over the horizon.

"What do you say we grab some dinner, and I'll explain why you're a numbskull and how you're going to fix this?" Mickey flashed a smile, his perfect white teeth glowing in the fading light, and Hank had a sinking feeling he would regret spilling his guts.

"Sure. Where do you want to eat?"

"Anywhere that serves crow."

A definite mistake. Mickey would haul him through the wringer before they finished their meal, and Hank had no one to blame but himself.

SADIE ROSE at dawn the next morning, and she and Sweet Pea went straight to her office. She'd just poured herself a cup of coffee when the bell chimed. She went downstairs and found her new volunteer decked out in green pants and a green plaid blouse with Christmas trees dangling from her earlobes, Prancer cradled in her arms.

Seeing Jody brought a smile to Sadie's lips, and a Christmas carol to her ears. "Coffee?"

Jody smiled, twin dimples flashing.

Sadie added a generous amount of sugar and cream. "Why don't we sit outside? The sunrises are spectacular here."

They sat in the rockers with the dogs curled at their feet, and Sadie said, "I didn't expect you so early. Few people are up this time of day."

Jody waved a dismissive hand, tiny Christmas trees painted on her nails. "Oh, Nicky and I are always up before dawn—year-round. We have so much to do we've got to get an early start." Her eyes sparkled with barely suppressed merriment. "Besides, if we weren't up before dawn, we'd miss the sunrises."

Sadie sipped her coffee, nodding her agreement. She loved the mornings, loved the quiet before the commuter traffic filled the air with the hustle and bustle of the city. It was a peaceful moment before her day began.

"I love to watch the sunsets, too," Sadie said. "But I have to admit I don't see as many in the spring and summer as I'd like because I'm falling into bed while it's still light outside. But I soak them up in the fall and winter since the sun sets so much earlier."

Jody nodded, gently rocking her chair. "The winter sunsets are spectacular, and we try to see all of them."

"That is something I love about the wintertime. And when the northern lights appear, there's just nothing like it."

"Oh yes, the northern lights are amazing." Jody sipped her

coffee, then got down to business. "So, what do you need me to do today?"

"For starters, I was hoping you could tackle Saturday Movie Night and the brunches, and the holiday schedule needs planning, too."

Jody clapped her hands, her face brimming with excitement. "Prancer and I would love to do that. The holidays are my favorite time of the year. Just show me where everything is, and I'll get right on it."

They finished their coffee, and Sadie led her through setting up movie night. When Jody started firing off ideas, Sadie relaxed, confident her new volunteer would have it all in hand so she could focus on the farm.

CHAPTER 5

S adie finished for the day—a sweaty, dirty mess with a sense of accomplishment that resonated deep within her. She loved farming, loved spending her days outdoors working the land. In some ways, the farm had become the family she'd lost, reminding her of the times she'd spent with her dad, working in the garden, studying nature.

Dusting off her hands, she headed to her office, then stopped in her tracks when she saw the porch.

OH MY GOD.

Orange lights weaved in and out of the spider webs filling the porch and eaves. A witch on a broom and a scarecrow perched on either side of the steps. The two pumpkins she'd put next to the door had been replaced with bales of straw and white, pink and orange pumpkins arranged in clusters, some carved and some not.

Her inner Grinch raised his head in protest that it was way too soon for holiday decorations of any kind. Sadie didn't hate the holiday season per se, but her decorating skills were minimal, and while she decorated the farm, she'd never done anything on this scale. She'd obviously inherited her father's Grinch gene.

For Christmas she hauled out the lights and strung them over the porch railing and put up a tree inside the deli, but inside her house, no decorations other than exterior lights and then only because her customers expected it.

There had been a time she'd loved the holidays and Christmas in particular—the entire holiday season—until she'd lost her parents her sophomore year in high school. Having no one to celebrate the holidays with sucked all the joy from it. Sure, her foster parents included her, but it just wasn't the same.

Sadie climbed the steps, marveling at the artfully decorated exterior.

Where had all the decorations come from?

She went inside, stilling the urge to demand answers. As much as she wasn't a fan, her customers would love it!

Jody greeted her as she entered the store, sparkly orange garland wrapped around her neck as she carved a ginormous pumpkin.

"What do you think?" Jody asked.

The Grinch snarled, and she tamped it down. "It's very Halloweenie," she offered with forced excitement. "Where did all this come from?"

Jody wiped her hands and went to the front window to plug in more orange lights shaped like pumpkins. "Oh, here and there."

"You've done a fabulous job," Sadie said.

Jody's pleasure shone brighter than the gapped tooth grin on her pumpkin. "I'm glad you like it. The day after Halloween, I'll get the Christmas decorations up."

"So soon?" Sadie asked.

Hands on hips, Jody shook a finger at her. "It's never too early. I've already started getting sign-ups for holiday decorating classes on everything from a master class on bow making and gift wrapping to holiday crafts. Can you think of a better way to get folks into the Christmas spirit than to have our holiday decorations up?"

Sadie couldn't deny that made sense, but it didn't mean she would join in, either.

Sweet Pea and Prancer played tug-of-war with a black rope and both had orange bows on their collars.

Sadie swallowed back her resistance to the decorations and forced a smile. "I'm calling it a day. I need to get ready for the Get the Word Out event. Will you be there?"

Jody grinned at her. "Oh, Nicky and I wouldn't miss it. And he'll be here any minute to pick me up. You go on, and I'll close up."

Sadie thanked her, collected Sweet Pea, and headed to the two-story farmhouse at the far end of the property to shower and change. Get the Word Out had become an annual event to educate the community on the services Job Hunters 4 You provided. Sadie donated food and volunteered to help feed the hundreds of people in attendance.

After she showered, swiped on some makeup, and slipped into jeans and a warm sweater, she fed Sweet Pea, then raced to the bus stop to catch the 590 across town. She had a pickup, but mostly used it for farm deliveries. For everything else, she preferred public transportation. It's where she'd met Annie and a host of other friends.

Twenty minutes later, she exited the bus and walked the two blocks to Job Hunters 4 You. Tables leaned against the building, waiting to be set up along with stacks and stacks of chairs.

Sadie picked up her pace and headed inside, weaving her way through the volunteers as she headed to the massive restaurant-sized kitchen where she found Annie hard at work.

She looked up, saw Sadie, and tossed her an apron. "How was your day?" Annie asked.

"Long, but good. It always is when I'm doing what I love." It was absolutely true. She loved farming, and all the hard work helped her forget the emptiness inside, especially during the holiday season. Long hours were part and parcel of the job, but it also made it easy to forget she had no family to celebrate the holidays with.

"How about you? How was your day?"

Annie sighed, releasing a weighted breath. "A bit challenging with a three-year-old. Zoe said she was hungry and wanted cheese. When I gave her a cheese stick, she said she wanted funny cheese. It took me twenty minutes to figure out she wanted Colby cheese."

The twinkle in her eyes told Sadie that even though she'd faced numerous frustrations, she'd loved every minute of it. "And how are you feeling?"

"Surprisingly good. No morning sickness." She quickly knocked on the butcher block cutting board with a sassy grin. "With Zoe, I was sick all the time. So far, this pregnancy has been nausea-free—a real blessing with a toddler in the house."

"Where is my little munchkin?"

"With Jack. I needed a break after chasing her around all day."

Sadie paused in her food preparations to give her friend a quick hug. "Keeping up with a preschooler is exhausting, isn't it?"

Annie leaned into her, smiling. "It is."

"She can always come to the farm if you need a break."

"Thanks. I may take you up on that."

They started putting a massive salad together. "By the way, I met some old friends of yours and apparently I'm on their need-to-help list."

Annie's brows quirked as she looked over at her. "Who?"

"Jody and Nick Claws."

Annie's eyes widened. "No way."

Sadie gave her a single swift nod. "Way. They showed up on

my doorstep two days ago, telling me they'd chosen my farm as their earlier-than-usual Christmas project."

"So, you're their other Christmas assignment. Let me guess, Jody and Prancer took over event planning for you."

Surprised, Sadie asked, "How did you know?"

"Because Jody is an event coordinator extraordinaire. You won't find anybody better."

Sadie couldn't disagree. In the two days she'd been there, Jody had the events well in order. "She is, but you said other project. What else is she doing?" Selfish as it sounded, she didn't want to share her miracle event coordinator.

Annie's grin widened. "Nick's helping in Hank's classroom. And you know what that means?"

The look on Annie's face gave her pause. "No, what?"

"That she and Nick have plans for you and Hank."

Ever since Annie's cousin, Hank, moved to Snowside, Annie had used every opportunity to sing his praises. It was bad enough having her best friend meddling in her love life, but it never occurred to her that Jody and Nick had arrived on her doorstep for anything more than to offer a helping hand. If they thought they'd set her up with Godzilla, they were in for a rude awakening because Sadie didn't have time for a relationship, even if they found her the perfect man—which Hank Dabrowski was not!

"What exactly did Nick and Jody do the last time they were here?"

"Oh my gosh, where to begin? Jody ran the entire show for Jack in terms of fundraising. She literally put Jobs Hunters 4 You on the map with her events. People still talk about the flash mob we did at the mall."

Sadie had heard about that, but she hadn't been able to attend. She'd seen the video Annie's nephew, Tony, had recorded and couldn't deny it was amazing. "Tell me more."

Annie finished cutting the last of the veggies and pursed her lips in thought. "Nick helped wherever Jack needed him, whether it was stocking shelves or working with clients. Be forewarned, those two are tricky. They know how to persuade people to do things they'd never planned on doing." A crooked grin made Annie's eyes sparkle with delight at the memory. "She got me to do a scavenger hunt at Jobs Hunters 4 You for the Christmas dinner. She also got me to volunteer as a server for their annual Christmas meal."

Annie dumped the vegetables into the massive metal bowl, then winked at Sadie. "That pair are quite the marriage brokers, too, as Herman would say."

Herman rode Annie's bus until he moved in with his daughter. A gruff exterior, but warm and fuzzy inside, he'd befriended Sadie when she started riding the bus.

"How so?" Sadie asked, needing as much information as possible to ward off any matchmaking attempts the two might have up their sleeves.

"Jack took me to Jeremy's Old Time Christmas Tree Farm for a sleigh ride, and Nick and Jody showed up to drive the sleigh."

"Why is that odd?" Sadie asked.

"Mainly because Jeremy didn't know them. They weren't supposed to be our drivers, but somehow they knew we would be there, got the sleigh, and drove it."

Suspicion blossomed inside Sadie. If this was part of their routine, she'd be sure and set Jody straight about her and Hank first thing tomorrow morning.

"Did they do anything else?"

"Well, Tony has never confirmed this, but I'm pretty sure that Nick is the one who got him to believe in miracles again. Let me tell you, that kid gave up on Santa Claus at a very young age. I don't know what Nick said or did, but he made Tony a believer in Santa."

It sounded more and more like a Hallmark movie. They might

have convinced a teenager to believe in holiday magic, but they wouldn't sway Sadie.

"And Jody oh-so-subtly left the information on Jack's desk about a Christmas scavenger hunt." Annie wagged a finger. "Those two are devious, but have the biggest hearts of anyone I know. You're lucky to have them in your corner."

Even with Annie's assurances, Sadie would reserve judgment until after she'd actually worked with them.

Sadie picked up the platter of veggies to take to the walk-in cooler. "By the way, Jody said she and Nick would be here to help tonight."

The brilliance of Annie's smile put Jody's Halloween lights to shame. "Oh, that's wonderful. I can't wait to introduce them to Zoe."

Sadie went into the cooler, and Annie called out, asking her to bring a bag of carrots. She set the tray on the shelf, grabbed the carrots, and started back when she heard, "What's up, Buttercup?"

Annie's gurgle of laughter, then, "Taking a trip through the tulips, Puddin' Pop."

Low male laughter echoed in response. Not just any male— her arch nemesis, Hank *Godzilla* Dabrowski! He stood beside Annie sampling one of the deviled eggs.

Sadie wanted desperately to dash back into the cooler and lock herself away until Hank left, but she didn't run from anything, especially *Godzilla*.

Sucking it up, she set the carrots on the counter beside Annie.

Hank's vivid blue eyes swept over her with the same accusatory glare, the same distrust as the last time she'd seen him.

Annie swatted his arm. "Stop that. Sadie is a friend, so quit scowling at her."

Hank had the decency to flush. "Good to see you again, Sadie."

She remained stiff and unbending. "You, too."

Annie rolled her eyes. "You two are impossible!" She pulled off her apron and handed it to Hank. "Help Sadie cut up the carrots," she said, then marched out the door.

Another uncomfortable silence descended that broke when Sadie pushed the carrots toward him. "If you peel, I'll slice."

Hank grunted and began peeling.

Determined not to be the cause of their animosity, Sadie said, "So, how's Elroy? He hasn't been by in a while."

Hank cast a speculative glance at her, as if trying to determine an ulterior motive behind her inquiry. Finally, he hefted a shoulder. "Feisty as ever."

"That sounds like Elroy. Is he coming tonight?"

"He said he was."

His clipped response left Sadie scrambling for a topic to discuss. Choosing honesty over more mundane chitchat, she said, "I would never take advantage of Elroy."

The silence that followed was so charged, Sadie shifted from foot to foot.

Hank set down the peeler and faced her. "Maybe not, but that land is extremely valuable. I have to ensure he's not taken advantage of."

Speechless, Sadie could only stare at him. "Are you implying that I would do that? To the man who had befriended me, invited me to his holiday dinners so I wouldn't be alone? You've got a lot of nerve to insinuate such a thing."

Hank's piercing blue eyes stabbed her again.

Sadie took off her apron and threw it at him. "Since you think so little of me, I'll let you finish up here," she said, then stormed out.

CHAPTER 6

H ank watched Sadie march out of the kitchen, her green eyes hot and furious. His fault—again.

He'd just finished with the carrots when Mickey stuck his head in the door. "Hey, Godzilla, I need help setting up tables."

Hank shot him a mock scowl at the use of the nickname Sadie had given him. It wasn't a nickname he minded, unless Sadie used it in a voice dripping with disdain. Then again, he really did like her all fired up over him.

Pushing thoughts of the woman aside, he followed Mickey into the dining room and began setting up tables. No matter how hard he focused on the job at hand, his mind strayed back to his argument with Sadie.

He'd intended to apologize as he'd promised his uncle, and so far he had two botched attempts under his belt. The last time, she'd shoved the flowers in his face. The woman had a temper as volatile as those expressive green eyes.

Why couldn't she listen to reason? It wasn't personal. He was only trying to protect his uncle just like he'd done with his mother. If he hadn't stepped in, his mom would have lost the pub their family had owned for decades, and to someone he trusted —his ex.

"I expected you here an hour ago," Mickey said, bringing him back to the present.

"Sorry, got delayed at work."

"Because you're late, you're on cleanup duty."

Hank laughed, shaking off the last remnant of work. "So, besides cleanup, what else do you need me to do?" he asked, as they set up the last table.

Mickey handed him an apron and a serving spoon. For the next hour, Hank served food and extolled all the wonderful services Job Hunters 4 You provided to the public. If the overflowing donation buckets were any indication, Get the Word Out was a huge success.

Hank thoroughly enjoyed himself, except for the times he caught sight of Sadie and anger threatened to boil over, but if he were totally honest with himself, something more simmered below the surface, something that felt a lot like attraction.

SADIE HAD JUST FINISHED HELPING clean the kitchen and was about to head home when Annie insisted she come upstairs and join them on the roof for the after-hours party she and Jack had put together for the volunteers. Sadie wanted to plead exhaustion and head home, but she really wanted to spend time with her friends. She could catch up on sleep anytime, so instead of leaving, she followed Annie upstairs to the apartment Jack had lived in before they were married and where Mickey lived now.

After pouring her a glass of wine, Annie shooed Sadie up to the roof while she checked on Zoe. The three-year-old had fallen asleep more than an hour ago, exhausted.

Sadie took the stairs to the roof and wandered over to stare out at the river, watching as it gurgled past. She loved this view of the city and never tired of it.

"I'm jealous every time I come up here," a familiar voice murmured beside her.

Sadie stiffened, then cast a sidelong glance at Godzilla. She should've known he'd be here since he and Mickey were best buds, not to mention Annie's cousin.

"The view is beautiful," she admitted.

His dark gaze held hers with the same intensity as when he'd accused her of trying to buy Elroy's land for pennies on the dollar. She flinched at the memory. She didn't appreciate being labeled an opportunist. Even though Annie, Jack, and Mickey insisted he was truly a nice guy, he'd yet to show that side of himself to her.

"Have I got something stuck in my teeth?" she asked to ease the tension building within her.

A blank expression crossed his face. "No, why would you think that?"

"With the way you're staring at me, I assumed something was wrong."

"I want to discuss the sale of the property with you."

Sadie bristled. Not this again! "I already told you to talk to Elroy."

"He won't listen to me."

Big surprise.

Sadie squared her shoulders. "Do you have some reason to believe he's incapable of making this decision?"

"No. But he's soft-hearted."

Anger sizzled. "So you think I'd take advantage of that?"

"That's a strong word."

Sadie eyed him. "But accurate."

Before he could respond, Jody threw an arm around each of them. "Two of my favorite people. I'm so glad to see you both here tonight. I love Job Hunters 4 You."

Sadie forced a smile. "What Jack and Mickey do here is absolutely amazing."

"It's people like you who've made them a success. They wouldn't be here without the support of their friends," Jody said.

"From what I hear, you and Nick played a big part in it."

Jody waved a hand in dismissal. "We just helped out here and there. They're the ones who made it a success."

Hank remained unusually silent, which was out of character. In Sadie's experience, the man never hesitated to share his opinions.

"I think I'll get another beer," he said at last. "Can I get you ladies anything?"

"I'm good, thanks," Sadie said.

Jody's gaze darted between the two of them. "I heard there are hot toddies. I wouldn't turn that down."

Hank smiled. "Coming right up."

Sadie watched him walk away, grateful for the reprieve. The man was more annoying than the Class-A noxious weeds she fought on her farm.

HANK CURSED himself for being such an idiot as he headed over to the makeshift bar where Mickey served drinks.

Why did he find it necessary to continually antagonize Sadie?

Because she pushes your buttons with just a look.

Maybe he'd been a tad overprotective of Elroy, but his great-uncle was generous to a fault, and Hank feared some unscrupulous person would swindle him. Rage filled him again. If his mom hadn't told him about Lydia's plans, she would have purchased the property far under market value. And that was the woman he'd thought he'd loved. He didn't even know Sadie McCluskey.

But insinuating she had less than pure motives hadn't been his finest moment and clearly the wrong approach, as he'd pissed off both Sadie and Elroy. In his defense, he hadn't found out until just recently that Sadie had insisted on paying fair market value for the land.

Mickey shook a finger at him, interrupting the thoughts ping-ponging in his head. "All work and no play makes Hank a cranky boy," he sing-songed.

Hank couldn't deny the truth of his words. Time to relax, and enjoy the evening, since he'd done nothing for himself in a long time, and maybe that was intentional. If he kept busy thinking about others, it made it easier to forget about his personal life—or lack of.

"I'm here, aren't I?" he said.

Mickey studied him closely—to the point Hank looked away.

"In body, but not spirit," Mickey said.

Bull's-eye. Mickey could read him like no one else, just as he'd done when they'd been in Afghanistan. And he never hesitated to remind Hank the team depended on him to have his head in the game.

"I'm right here, and I'm paying attention."

Mickey studied him. "Only because I called you on it. We need a night out where you forget about work and just have fun—tomorrow night at my place. I'll cook dinner, and we'll watch the game."

"What are you cooking?"

"New recipe."

"I'll bring the appetizer," Hank said to ensure they'd have one edible dish because while Mickey was an amazing cook, his new recipes were iffy at best.

"You're bringing the beer, too. Your problem, your alcohol."

The tension that knotted his shoulders eased. An evening with Mickey was just what he needed.

＊

"WELL, WHAT DO YOU THINK?" Jody asked her husband.

Nick cut a brief glance her direction. "I think it's just like I told you in the beginning—it's going to be a challenge to bring these two together."

Jody stroked Prancer as she thought over his comment. "I agree, but we have a little more time than we normally do."

"We do, but…"

"But what?" Jody asked when he didn't continue.

"I think there's more going on between these two. I mean, Hank would have to be an absolute idiot at this point not to realize that Sadie had no plans to take advantage of Elroy. And he knows she's offered Elroy far more than he asked for the property."

Jody nodded. "I was thinking the same thing. He's being a typical male who stuck his foot in his mouth and doesn't know how to remove it."

"And how do you propose he do that?" Nick asked, arching a bushy white brow at her as he turned onto the interstate.

"By groveling, of course."

"He's apologized twice."

Jody's expression turned resolute as she shook a finger at Nick. "Don't tell me you call those lame attempts apologies."

"He attempted to, then messed it up."

She caught the hint of a smile under Nick's full white beard. Rather than comment on it, she said, "So, what's our next move?"

"We bring them together, of course."

She'd taught him well. "You're absolutely right." Jody rubbed her hands in gleeful anticipation. "Have I got an idea for you!"

CHAPTER 7

T wo weeks before Halloween, Sadie worked the field farthest from the store in close proximity to the greenhouse. She shivered as the breeze passed over her. Wrapping the scarf more snugly around her neck, she continued to clear out the raised beds of wilted tomato plants. Smiling at the prospect of a new crop of tomatoes and lettuce in November with the hydroponic system made her unaccountably happy.

Checking her watch, she realized it was time to get cleaned up for the farm tour Jody had scheduled with a local kindergarten class, and she'd promised to lead the tour.

This was her favorite type of farm tour, and Jody had put together some fantastic hands-on crafts for the kids. Jody had told her there was also a little girl in a wheelchair, another reason the teacher had chosen her farm because it was handicapped accessible from the barn to the fields to the wagons.

Sadie's motto—farming needed to be experienced by everyone.

Backing the motorized wooden hay wagon out of the barn, she drove it to the deli and parked it, then attached the ramps. Long wooden seats lined both sides of the wagon with openings on both ends for wheelchairs. When she had it all set up, she went to her office and freshened up, wearing her typical work clothes because she wanted the children to see her in her usual attire, right down to the calluses on her palms, proof-positive she spent her days in the field.

She found Jody at her desk, going over what Sadie assumed was the program for today, but rather than talk to Jody, she made a detour to the deli where the line of customers nearly reached the door, and Dale raced between taking and preparing orders.

Sadie stepped behind the deli case, scribbling orders and filling drinks. Ten minutes later, Jody waved her over.

"I've got this, now," Dale said. "Go take care of the farm tour."

"I'll be back to help as soon as I can," Sadie promised.

Sadie took the clipboard Jody handed her. "We can't keep kindergartners waiting. Their little bodies need to be moving. You take care of the tour, and I'll help Dale at the counter. I see now I should've scheduled this later in the day or earlier in the morning. Didn't have my thinking cap on."

Sadie hurried outside, Sweet Pea on her heels to find Nick surrounded by a group of five-year-olds all vying for his attention.

"Are you sure you're not Santa Claus?" a little boy asked, turning his head side-to-side as he inspected his beard.

Nick's hearty chuckle echoed over him, his eyes twinkling with merriment. "What do you think?"

The little boy shrugged, then reached up and tugged on his beard, which drew more laughter from him.

"My beard is definitely real." He patted his stomach. "So is my belly."

A little girl in a wheelchair with bright blue eyes stared at his middle. "And it jiggles like a bowlful of jelly."

Nick slapped his thigh, releasing another bellowing laugh. "That it does, Kirstin, that it does."

What was Nick doing here?

Annie's words came back to her. "He's helping out with Hank's class."

Had Jody set her up to give Hank's class a tour? If that was the case, where was Hank?

A dark-haired woman who Sadie guessed was somewhere in her forties gathered the children together. "Okay, kids, we're about to begin."

Sadie went over to her and introduced herself. "Hi, I'm Sadie McCluskey, owner of McCluskey River Farm, and I'm so glad you and your class are with us today."

"Rosario Garcia, Mr. Dabrowski's aide."

The dull throb of a headache pulsed in Sadie's forehead as she realized she'd be dealing with Godzilla and had been set up by Jody and Nick.

She straightened her shoulders. Just because Hank behaved like a jerk didn't mean she couldn't suck it up and make it a memorable day for his students.

"Where is Mr. Dabrowski?"

"Inside." Rosario leaned closer, dropping her voice. "One of our little guys had an accident, and he's getting him cleaned up."

Sadie absorbed the information, trying not to feel a shift in her feelings for him after her unkind thoughts a moment ago, but it was impossible to ignore the admiration building inside her. It took a certain type of person to teach kindergartners.

"They should be back shortly. I'm sorry for the delay."

Sadie waved off her apology. "It's no problem. We're very laid-back here."

Rosario smiled and was about to say something more when she rushed off to the deal with a pair of boys about to come to blows.

Sadie turned to check on the wagon and make sure everything was in order when Sweet Pea let out a low whine. She looked back to find Hank at her side, a little boy holding his hand, his eyes red. His forlorn expression sent an ache straight into her heart.

She pushed her annoyance with Godzilla aside and focused on the little boy. Squatting down to his level, she smiled and held out her hand. "Hi, I'm Sadie McCluskey. Welcome to McCluskey River Farm."

The little boy shrank back.

Hank's voice whispered over her, and a frission of awareness rippled over her. "Bobby doesn't like to shake hands."

Not missing a beat, Sadie said, "That's no problem at all. We all have different things we like and don't like. Isn't that right, Bobby?"

His eyes widened as if he'd expected anger. The tension in his face transformed into a hesitant smile. "That's what Mr. D tells us, too," Bobby said, adoring eyes gazing up at his teacher.

"I think you have a very smart teacher," Sadie said.

Bobby gave her a single, swift nod.

Sadie leaned forward with a stage whisper just loud enough for Bobby to hear and asked, "Would you be interested in helping me drive the wagon?"

Something akin to worship filled Bobby's eyes. He looked from Hank to Sadie, then asked, "Really, I could do that?"

Sadie glanced at Hank, who gave a subtle nod of agreement.

"Absolutely."

The sparkle in Bobby's eyes dimmed. "I always sit with my friend, Kirstin. I can't leave her alone."

"There should be plenty of room for two as the front can accommodate three people. We could always trade-off, too. That way, everyone gets a chance to ride in front."

Bobby nodded vigorously.

After they got Bobby and Kirstin situated, then the rest of the children settled, they set off, Sweet Pea trotting alongside the wagon. Sadie took the children out to pick the last of the vegetables—rutabagas, turnips, winter squash and potatoes. She'd left enough in the ground for kids to finish harvesting them. They'd scrambled from the wagon with shouts and hoots of laughter as she showed them how to pick them. Not a one had been squeamish about digging in the dirt. If anything, the complete opposite.

Taking the wicker baskets from the wagon, the children filled them with as much dirt as produce. Sadie explained how the crops were planted and how long it took them to grow. When they finished, they loaded the children and baskets back into the wagon and headed to the greenhouse.

She led them inside, where several hydroponic crops were close to harvest. They oohed and awed over the plants, leaning in to see the cluster of roots floating in water.

She pushed Kirstin's wheelchair to the strawberry plants.

When the children had gathered around, Sadie said, "This greenhouse has a special type of heating called geothermal to keep it warm in the winter. Geothermal is heat produced in the earth, and it's used to heat the greenhouse, so plants can grow here all year long."

Several of the children giggled and fidgeted, a clear sign they were growing bored.

"Who's ready to go outside and pick pumpkins?"

A dozen hands shot up along with shouts of *me, me, me*! She took them back outside, Kirstin rolling along behind her. The walkway had been designed for handicap accessibility as part of her *You Pick* farm plan.

The kids raced up and down the rows and once they'd each chosen a pumpkin, Sadie took them to the tiny petting zoo at the opposite end of the farm to see the animals, collect eggs, and feed the chickens. Their excited chatter filled her heart with joy.

"Rabbits are better pets than goats," a redhead with a button nose and flashing green eyes told the little boy next to her.

"Nah-ah! Goats are the best because they can climb, and jump, and run," a boy with floppy curls insisted.

"Kittens are the best," another said, snuggling a smoky-colored kitten to her cheek.

Rather than take sides, Sadie said, "The great thing about all the animals is, they each have special qualities to love just like each of you, but there is nothing more special than baby animals." She pressed a finger to her lips and motioned them over to the hay stacked in the corner.

Excited squeals erupted when she showed them the litter of kittens, their eyes tightly sealed. "These babies are too little to hold. Does anyone know why?"

Several hands shot up, and she pointed to the little boy with the mop of curly hair, standing beside Rosario. She seemed to recall his name was Tommy.

"Because they need to be close to their mama," he said.

"That's exactly right, Tommy. Tiny babies need their mamas, and it also upsets their mamas if we handle their babies." She pointed to the kitten Tommy clutched to his chest. "But this kitten is older and loves to be held and cuddled."

Another little boy named Henry hovered beside Kirstin, quietly protective of her. Sadie felt an immediate connection with him. She'd watched him hand her a kitten. When Kirstin's delighted laughter rang out, Henry's smile lit up the barn's dingy interior.

"Would you like to hold the bunny?" she asked him. She held out a lop-eared black bunny. When he didn't respond, she said, "I promise she loves children. Can you guess what her name is?"

Henry tentatively stroked a floppy ear.

Sadie leaned in closer so only Henry could hear. "Her name is Bubbles."

Henry's mouth formed a surprised O, then he smiled, and Sadie had never seen anything so beautiful in her life.

"Why do you call her Bubbles?"

Sadie slid Bubbles into his arms. "Because whenever she sees a carrot, she blows bubbles." Sadie removed a carrot from her pocket and handed it to Henry.

"I can feed her?"

Sadie nodded, a wave of tenderness coming over her as she watched Henry hold out the carrot and right on cue, Bubbles blew bubbles. His deep belly laugh was infectious, and the other children gathered around, watching her squirm and blow more bubbles as Henry held the carrot out to her.

When Bubbles finished her treat, the children scattered to play with the other animals. Sadie glanced up and found Hank's eyes on her, watching her closely, and suddenly the drafty barn felt smoldering hot from just the intensity of his gaze.

CHAPTER 8

Once the children had their snacks that Jody put together, Sadie offered Hank, Rosaria, and Nick coffee. At their nod, she poured them each a cup. By the time the kids finished eating, Hank announced they'd be leaving in ten minutes.

Plenty of whining and complaining followed, but Hank took it all in stride, telling them they couldn't miss the bus.

Sadie stepped up and drew their attention. "Miss Jody and I are so thrilled you came to visit us today, especially our animals." She pointed at Bubbles, fast asleep in Henry's arms. "And because we've had such a good time, we're sending you home with tickets for a special children's Christmas movie just for you and your families here on the farm in December."

Whoops of joy filled the room as Sadie handed the tickets to Hank. "These are family passes for parents, brothers, sisters, and grandparents."

Hank took her hand and squeezed it. Sadie's pulse jumped as she looked into his steady gaze.

"I can't tell you how much this means to them." He lowered his voice. "Most of my students have very little money, and their parents can barely afford to provide for their basic needs. This will make such a difference for them. Thank you."

Those were the nicest words he'd ever said to her.

"I'm happy to do it."

"How do you make money doing that?"

"I don't. It's not my intent to profit from movie night. It's about bringing families to the farm. Some of them will eventually buy produce from me, or come here for lunch, or refer a friend. Of course, some won't, but that's okay, too. This place is more than just a farm." She hadn't intended it as a dig at him, but when he winced, she realized he'd taken it that way.

"That comment wasn't directed at you. I was just sharing how I feel."

Hank was silent for a moment, his hypnotic blue eyes scrutinizing her. "I know that wasn't your intent, but the fact is, I deserved it. You were right the other night at Jack and Annie's. I misjudged your intentions with Elroy."

"You did."

"I see that now."

Sadie studied the fine lines bracketing his eyes and wondered if he finally understood, but she remained wary. He'd apologized before—twice—but this time seemed sincere, rather than forced.

"Thank you."

She'd seen a side of Hank today that she'd never seen before —the caring, thoughtful, dedicated teacher. This new Hank intrigued her, made her want to know more about him. Could she have been as wrong about him as he'd been about her?

His expression flashed gratitude and something more that Sadie couldn't define, and it left her feeling like melted caramel inside.

More grumblings arose as Rosario started guiding the children to the bus.

Sadie leaned toward Hank, so only he could hear her. "I could bring the rabbits and kittens to your classroom for the kids to see again."

His smile sent a mad fluttering through her belly.

"Thank you," he mouthed, then whistled to get the kids' attention. "Listen up. Miss Sadie just told me she brings some of the smaller animals to classrooms, and she'd be willing to do that for our class."

"Even Bubbles?" Henry asked.

"Especially Bubbles. She loves seeing kids. But it's usually only bunnies and kittens—not the chickens."

"When can you bring them?" Kirstin asked.

"Miss Sadie and I are working that out," Hank said.

"Can you bring more of your snacks, too?" Barbie asked, in a voice so quiet Sadie had to strain to hear her.

"Absolutely. Animals and snacks," Sadie said.

The complaints vanished, and the children headed for the bus jabbering about movie night on the farm and when Sadie would bring the animals to school.

Sadie watched them leave, telling herself this was something she did for every group, but deep down she knew it was more than that. She'd wanted an excuse to see Hank Dabrowski again.

CHAPTER 9

Hank couldn't imagine what he'd been thinking when he agreed to have Sadie bring the animals to his class. He and Sadie got along like bathtubs and hairdryers and had from the moment they met.

Could part of their antagonism arise from his attraction to her? That thought stopped him cold.

Was it possible this whole mess had started because subconsciously he'd been protecting himself from Sadie and another heartbreak?

He couldn't deny the possibility. Maybe it was time he stopped worrying about the past and opened himself up to someone new. He just hoped his pig-headedness hadn't destroyed any possibility of a relationship with Sadie.

Hank finished cleaning the classroom, locked the door, and headed to see his uncle Elroy. Elroy lived in a small detached home on the east side of Snowside—the same place he and Aunt Myra had lived for almost 50 years until her death two years ago. Hank pulled up in front and stared at the exterior.

He'd spent many weekends working on everything from

plumbing to electrical, and it had been a struggle just to get Elroy's agreement to the minor fixes. His uncle was proud and insisted on doing most of the repairs himself.

Hank sighed, pushed open the truck door and went up the porch steps. Tapping on the front door, he pushed it open, calling out to Elroy.

No response.

He headed for the kitchen, calling his name again.

Silence.

Hank opened the back door, expecting to find Elroy sitting in front of the firepit sipping a beer, but the chairs were empty and no fire.

His gaze circled the yard.

Empty.

He turned to head inside, then stopped when he saw Elroy high on a ladder, cleaning leaves out of the gutter.

Hank shook his head, but didn't chastise his uncle. Everyone else in the family would, but not Hank. He understood the need for independence and wouldn't deprive Elroy of it. Yes, he might fall, but that was his choice to make. Now, trying to explain that logic to his mother might be another story.

"You about done? I'm starving and you promised me dinner and beer."

Elroy shot him a mock scowl. "That stomach of yours is bigger than the Milky Way." He threw down a handful of leaves. "I'll be finished in a jiffy. Light the fire and grab some beer while I finish up."

Hank followed his directive and got the fire going, then grabbed two beers from the fridge and carried them outside. Perching a hip on the picnic table, he twisted the top off his beer as he watched Elroy work, teasing, "This isn't a bad job."

Elroy's chuckle carried over the yard. "You're a real comedian," he grumbled, but the twinkle in his eye said otherwise as he started down the ladder.

He accepted the beer Hank held out, taking a long, hearty sip, then plopped down into the chair next to the fire.

Hank took another sip of his beer. "You know Mom will have a fit if she hears you're climbing ladders."

"Who the hell's going to tell her?"

His surly response drew a snort from Hank as he eased into the chair beside him. "My lips are sealed. What you do here is your business."

The tension left Elroy's shoulders. "You're a good man. Clearly, I taught you well."

They sat in comfortable silence, listening as the wind gusted, sending leaves swirling over the patio. A flock of geese flew overhead in a wide V.

"So, how are those kiddos of yours doing?"

Hank smiled. He loved talking about his kids. "As far as teaching goes, they're great. They soak up everything with plenty of enthusiasm. I just wish—"

When he didn't continue, Elroy asked, "You just wish what?"

Hank studied his beer bottle as if the answers he searched for would magically appear. "I just wish I could do more to improve their lives."

"Don't you do that by teaching them?"

Hank waved a hand in dismissal. "Of course, but their needs go beyond teaching."

"Like what?"

"Like housing for one."

"You know, there's only so much you can do," Elroy said.

Yet, it never felt like enough.

Elroy took another sip of his beer as he contemplated Hank's concerns. "Obviously, you think you should do more, so do you have any ideas on how to fix the problem?"

His uncle read him like a book. "I've been going to city council meetings and urging them to make affordable housing a priority, but so far all they give me is lip service."

Elroy barked out a laugh. "I've monitored Snowside City Council for decades and here's what I've learned." He leaned forward and spoke in a conspiratorial whisper. "New members get elected, each hoping to make big, sweeping changes, but in my experience, nothing changes without public pressure. Their standard response is, we'll research it, and then they take their own sweet time before making a decision—" Elroy directed a meaningful look at Hank "—unless, of course, somebody puts their feet to the fire."

Hank pointed his beer bottle at him. "What have you got in mind?"

A devious smile slid over Elroy's face. "Well, I've been thinking that maybe we need the assistance of a contractor to put pressure on them."

"Do you have someone in mind?"

"Actually, I do. The man who remodeled Job Hunters 4 You. I think this is something that would be right up his alley."

Hank mulled over his idea. "I like it. I'll reach out to him and see if he's willing to join forces with me and get the council to take action."

Elroy gave a single swift nod. "Excellent. Now let's talk about your social life."

Leave it to Elroy to turn on a dime and put Hank in the hot seat about his love life, or the lack thereof. "Don't you have something better to worry about?"

"Oh, hell no. I'm an old man. I want to live vicariously through you. Are you dating anyone?"

Hank toyed with the label on the bottle, buying himself some time, but he knew it was useless. Elroy would poke and prod until he provided him with answers. "If you're asking if I'm dating anyone seriously, the answer is no."

Elroy's brows arched into a single line. "Are you dating anyone un-seriously?"

Hank huffed out a laugh. "Are you asking if I'm having one-night stands?"

"It wouldn't shock me if you were," Elroy said. "Are you?"

His uncle's tart remark made Hank laugh this time. "No, I'm not."

"Why the hell not? You're a young, healthy, relatively good-looking guy. You should be out having some fun, sewing some wild oats."

This was not a subject Hank wanted to discuss with his great-uncle, so he tried for a change of subject. "What's been going on with you?"

"You really think you can divert me that easily?" Elroy shook his head. "You're going to have to do better than that."

Hank took another long pull of his beer. "I'm not seeing anyone."

Elroy's silence was more disturbing than his twenty questions routine. "I admire the work you do, how much you care about your students, and how hard you strive to help them. Sally told me what Lydia did, but it's time to face facts—she wasn't the right woman for you. You know that as well as I do. I know that breakup hurt you, but it was the best thing that could have happened. It brought you to Snowside, and I'm grateful to have you here. You can't be afraid the next woman you get involved with is going to break your trust and your heart. Learn from your mistakes. Find a woman who's suited to you. You'll have rough patches, but it will end up much better than it did with Lydia."

Hank fingered Sadie's card in his pocket. He hadn't called and set a date for her to bring the animals to class. If he told Elroy about it, he would push for him to invite her to dinner, but Hank wasn't ready for that.

Are you sure?

"Did the kiddos enjoy the trip to the farm today?"

Elroy was on top of everything. "I'm not even going to ask how you knew we were at the farm today because nothing shocks me anymore where you're concerned. You have sources everywhere."

Elroy offered him a cheesy grin. "I know a few people here and there. I keep up. While I might be old, I'm not blind or stupid. So answer my question. How did the farm tour go?"

"It went really well, as I'm certain you already know, since you were the one who suggested I take the kids there, I'm assuming you also knew about the retrofitting Sadie did for handicapped accessibility."

"I did. I drew up the plans for her."

His uncle had spent his entire adult life working as an architect, and before he retired, he'd spearheaded handicap accessibility throughout the city, mainly because Aunt Myra had been wheelchair bound for the last ten years of their marriage.

"I should've known you'd had a hand in it."

"It's in my blood."

"Did you help her make the wagon wheelchair accessible, too?"

Elroy's chest thrust forward with pride. "I did. We hunted around and found what we needed. When the guy we bought the equipment from found out what we were doing, he donated it. Just so happened he had a nephew in a wheelchair. A lot of what she's done has been through donations or grants. Maybe you can understand why I wanted to give her the property at a reduced price."

Shame swept over him. He'd judged Sadie unfairly. He'd

made assumptions without determining the facts, and he'd judged her harshly because he'd compared her to Lydia.

Hank needed a change of subject. "I'm starving. What's for dinner?"

His uncle looked ready to press him further, but instead shrugged and went inside to start dinner, much to Hank's relief. He wasn't ready to probe his feelings for Sadie, and Elroy would prod him like a red-hot poker.

CHAPTER 10

S adie finished pruning the fruit trees just as the last rays of sunlight faded away. The farm tour had taken a sizeable chunk of her day, so she'd spent the rest of the afternoon and evening in the field. But she'd rather work late than miss spending time with the children, even if it meant seeing Godzilla.

Her feelings toward him had softened today. She actually saw the Hank Annie and Elroy kept telling her about, not the Godzilla she'd locked horns with and resented. Maybe there was more to the man than she realized. Pushing thoughts of Hank aside, she went back to work.

Full darkness had settled over the farm by the time Sadie traipsed back to her house, Sweet Pea at her heels.

Reheating leftovers, she scarfed them down, then filled the old clawfoot tub and eased her aching body into the steaming water. Tired as she was, she loved the work she did, but there were times she wished she raised a monoculture crop so she'd have one crop to care for and harvest, but that wasn't the kind of farming she enjoyed.

She loved raising a variety of crops, and now, thanks to her hydroponic system, she grew vegetables year-round. Branching out into events had also been a smart business decision that included selling Christmas trees cut from Old Time Christmas Farm, to holiday-themed brunches, and a host of classes thanks to Jody. She had the farm headed in a whole new direction in less than a week.

The chores were never-ending, but Sadie loved it all.

She lit the candles on the tray laid across the tub and settled back against the rim with a deep sigh, enjoying the feel of the water lapping over her skin.

Her phone vibrated. She swiped the screen to read the text.

Sorry to text so late. Had dinner at Elroy's. Would still love to have you bring the animals to class. What's a good day and time for you?

Sadie smiled. So he hadn't given her the cold shoulder.

Rather than text back, she called him.

Hank answered on the first ring. "I was afraid you might be asleep, so I texted instead of calling."

The sound of his voice sent warmth curling through Sadie, from her cheeks to the tip of her toes. "Just got in from the field a little while ago."

Hank released a low whistle. "Those are some long hours."

"Some things can't wait."

"You gave up your afternoon for my kids instead of working?" he asked.

Sadie shifted, and the water sloshed over her. "Giving the next generation of potential farmers a tour is part and parcel of operating the farm. I'd much rather work late than miss out on that."

A beat of silence. "What are you doing?" he asked.

Sadie flushed, then decided he probably had a fairly good idea of where she was and what she was doing. Their conversation suddenly felt intimate, and her skin went from warm to blazing hot. "I'm in the bathtub. Why?"

※

HANK'S IMAGINATION went wild as he envisioned Sadie naked and soaking, steam rising over her glistening skin. They might've had altercations about Elroy's land, but he couldn't deny the woman fascinated him. He wanted to run his fingers through her brown tresses, his hands over that compact body honed from hours of physical labor. She'd fit perfectly in his arms, and just the thought of holding her made his pulse throb.

He focused on the call, rather than the sounds coming from her bath.

"How about bringing the animals next Thursday afternoon?"

Her silence echoed in his head like a ticking bomb, and he wondered if she'd changed her mind when he desperately wanted her to say yes. He wanted to spend time with her despite all the reasons he shouldn't.

"I know it was my idea to bring the animals to class, but do you think it's wise for us to spend time together?"

She voiced the questions running through his head. He chose honesty over subterfuge. He'd had enough of that with Lydia. "A couple weeks ago I'd have said no, but now—"

When he didn't continue, she asked, "What?"

Did he really want to admit he was attracted to her?

"Let's just say I made a rash judgment, and I'm sorry."

A beat of hesitation, then a very soft "Okay."

He smiled, anticipation pulsing through him. "Wonderful. Maybe we could start over. I'm Hank Dabrowski, and I teach kindergarten. And you are?"

Her warm laugh cut through the jumble of emotions swirling inside of him. "Sadie McCluskey, owner of McCluskey River Farm."

"It's a pleasure to meet you," he said. "See you next week?"

"Yes."

Hank's heart suddenly felt lighter than it had since the day he'd learned Lydia had been lying to him. And it was all thanks to Sadie McCluskey.

SADIE ARRIVED at the school after lunch on Thursday, and Nick helped her carry the animals into the classroom. All of her animals traveled well, but even so they were skittish, especially with all the excited chatter coming from a roomful of giddy five-year-olds.

Hank held up a finger, then a second, and a third, his code for silence, and the room went whisper quiet. "When everyone finds their seats, we will bring an animal to each table for you to hold and pet."

"I want a kitten," one child shouted.

"I want a bunny," said another.

"You will all get a chance to hold a bunny and a kitten," Hank assured them.

Twenty-five pairs of eyes lit with barely suppressed excitement.

"Now, remember," Hank continued. "We have to hold the animals gently so we don't hurt them. If we frighten them, they could claw because they're afraid and hurt you."

With an adult at each table to monitor the animals, Sadie passed out animals to Hank, Rosario, and Nick, then took a pair of bunnies to her table and gave the children carrots to feed them.

"Does anyone know what a boy and girl bunny are called?" Sadie asked the group.

A redheaded pixie raised her hand. "A buck and a doe, and a baby is called a kitten or kit."

Clearly, she knew her bunnies. "That's absolutely correct. Does anyone know what kind of food they eat?"

Henry's hand shot up. "Carrots!"

"That's correct. They like a lot of different vegetables, and they eat bark and herbs, too, plus they drink a lot of water—as much as a twenty-pound dog."

That elicited oohs and ahhs from the group.

"Did you know," Sadie continued, "that rabbits can see behind themselves without turning their heads. They have twenty-eight teeth that keep growing throughout their life, and they chew one hundred and twenty times a minute? Rabbits love to chew."

The kids listened in rapt attention as Sadie rattled off more fun facts about bunnies, then she did the same with the kittens. The last bell rang, and Sadie collected the animals. Nick helped her put them in their cages as Hank and Rosario led the children out to their parents.

"Thank you, Miss Sadie," they called out before they left.

Sadie smiled and waved goodbye. "What sweet kids," she commented to Nick when they were alone.

"They are," he agreed.

Hank returned as they finished loading all the animals in their cages. "I can't thank you enough for bringing the animals in today."

Nick elbowed him, and with a loud stage whisper said, "Give the woman a proper thanks and take her to dinner."

Dark red splotches spread over Hank's cheeks that Sadie found adorable.

Before Hank could respond, Nick disappeared out the door.

"Would you like to go to dinner?" Hank asked.

Sadie thought over his question for a long moment before responding. "You don't owe me anything. I was happy to bring the animals to your class."

"I know," he said. "But I'd like to. Are you free Saturday?"

Twin dimples flashed, sending desire rocketing through her.

Sadie considered his invitation for all of a second, then said, "Yes, I'd love to."

"Great. I'll call you with the details."

"That would be great."

The silence that followed was like trying to decide whether to kiss a guy after a first date. Finally, Sadie said, "I'd better get these guys home."

He helped her carry them to her truck. She waved goodbye and headed to the farm, her spirits high. She had a date with *Godzilla* on Saturday. Would wonders ever cease?

SADIE FINISHED WORKING in the field and went to find Jody to see how plans were progressing for movie night, but Jody was nowhere to be found. Seeing Dale behind the deli counter, she went over to her. "Have you seen Jody?"

Busy preparing for the lunch rush, Dale pointed toward the barn. "She said she had to check on some things for movie night."

Sadie waved goodbye, promising to be back within the hour to help.

A moment later, she stepped into the barn and found Jody busily arranging tables. Pausing, she took in the setup and loved the changes. There were groupings of tables for families, sofas for couples on a romantic evening, and even a kids' section with beanbag chairs. It was perfect.

"This looks amazing."

Jody's grin was infectious. "You like it?"

"What's not to like? I love it!"

"I'm so glad."

"You said there were some things you needed to go over with me."

"I do. First, the snack bar. What do you think about changing up the menu?"

It definitely needed sprucing up. "What do you have in mind?"

"After the farm tour with Hank's class, I thought we could incorporate more food from the farm, and if it's well received, it could encourage sales. A double bang for the buck, so to speak."

"I think that's an excellent idea. I wish I'd thought of it months ago."

Jody waved off her comment. "You have enough on your plate without dealing with this."

"I still think it's brilliant."

Jody rushed on, ignoring the compliment. "I have another idea I want to propose."

"Fire away."

"What do you think about a themed dinner night?"

"Themed how?"

"I was thinking about how popular your grief group is and that you should expand and have a single ladies' night, or a speed dating night, or boys' night out."

Sadie considered her suggestions. "Do you really think people would come here for that?"

"Why wouldn't they?"

"We're in the city. They have so much to do already."

"They do, but this would be something entirely different. It would be something new that the young people are always craving, but I was also thinking you should have a fifty and up night, and maybe a seventy and up night. There's lots of lonely people out there."

Sadie liked the idea a lot. "Let's start with the ladies' night and see how it goes."

"I'll get right on it. I really think this is going to be a huge hit, and we can make it a holiday kickoff for next weekend. I'll have the Halloween decorations down, and the Christmas decorations up by then."

"Christmas in November?"

"Absolutely."

That seemed so early to have Christmas decorations out. Sadie turned to leave, but Jody stopped her with a hand on her arm.

"Nicky and I have been discussing new ways to draw in families. What do you think about having a Christmas carnival—Christmas on Ice? Provided we have snow, we could have snow angel contests, pin the nose on Rudolph, Santa Says, and booths with face painting and cookie decorating, and we could rent out booth space to help pay for this, plus I'll get donations of money and volunteers."

Sadie thought over her suggestions. "I swear you have the best ideas. Of course I'm in, and I love the whole concept."

A Christmas carnival here for kids and their families sent a spear of happiness straight to her heart, and she wanted to help any way she could. And knowing Jody, it would be a huge success.

"One more thing, and then I'll let you go. Were you satisfied with the school tour we did?"

"It was perfect."

"Does that mean you're open to more?"

Sadie hesitated. "I am, but I don't know that I'll have time to give all the tours."

"I'll work on scheduling some more, and I'll check with you before I finalize anything. How about that?"

Sadie smiled. "Sounds great." She turned to head back to the deli.

Jody called after her, "I hear you and Hank are going on a date tomorrow night."

Nothing got past the woman, and from what Annie had told her, she suspected she'd had a hand in it. "Yes."

Jody's smile lit up the barn. "That Hank, he's one special guy, isn't he?"

Sadie continued outside as if she hadn't heard her, but she couldn't deny the truth of Jody's statement.

CHAPTER 11

Hank had just gotten the kids settled at their tables and sat down at his desk for a break when Nick joined him. The man had worked out extremely well, much to his surprise. No question, he had a knack with children.

"What a morning! This group has more energy than three of me combined."

The twinkle in his eyes told Hank it wasn't a complaint, but a statement of fact. "I'm going to guess you've had some experience working with young children."

Nick's chuckle rumbled over him. "You could say that."

"Where else have you worked with them?"

Nick's eyebrows arched high onto his forehead as he pointed at his chest. "Looking at me, do you really have to ask that question?"

Hank laughed. "Point taken. I'm going to assume you've played Santa several times over the years?"

"Every single year for decades."

"What about grandkids?"

"Sadly, Jody and I couldn't have children of our own, so we've spent our lives helping others."

"What else do you and Jody do besides help those in need?"

Nick's wide grin made his eyes crinkle in the corners. "You name it, we do it. We make toys and travel the world, giving them away. Jody loves to bake, and I do wood carving."

"Where do you two call home?"

Nick's expression took on a mysterious glow. "Oh, we've got a place up north, and we've got a place in the east, but we mostly just bounce around. We like to stay on the move."

Before Hank could ask another question, Nick turned the tables on him. "So, what brought you to Snowside?"

How did he know about his recent move? He could have heard about it from Rosario, Annie, Jack, or Mickey, but he had the sense that Nick knew an awful lot about him without asking anyone.

"Angel Falls is a beautiful place," Nick continued. "Wasn't it difficult to leave, especially with all your family there?"

"Let me guess. You've been talking to Elroy, or was it Jack or Annie?"

Nick chuckled again, pretending to zip his lips. "I don't reveal my sources."

Not that Hank really cared. His life was an open book. "I felt the need for a change."

Nick nodded in understanding. "Breakups are hard. Sometimes a new place is the best medicine."

"I never said it was because of a breakup."

Nick braced his elbows on the desk, steepling his fingertips. "You didn't have to, it's obvious." He paused, then asked, "Where are you taking Sadie on Saturday?"

Hank stared at him. "How did you hear about our date?" He'd told no one except Sadie.

"A little birdie told me."

Hank gave up trying to wheedle information from the man. "I

haven't decided yet. I want to do something a little different to thank her for everything she's done for the kids."

"Something different?" Nick tugged on his ear, deep in thought. "You know what's always sounded like fun to me is kayaking the river to Drake Park and having a picnic."

Hank tried to picture Nick kayaking and couldn't. "Kayaking to Drake Park? That would be a lot of fun, but it's the end of October. It could be really cold, and I don't know if she kayaks."

"The weather is supposed to be in the seventies on Saturday."

"Really? That's usually warm for this time of year."

Nick gave him a single, swift nod. "It is and all the more reason to be outside enjoying the weather, don't you think?"

Hank couldn't disagree with him.

"I'll have Jody find out if she enjoys kayaking. She has a way of asking questions without giving away a surprise," Nick said.

Of that, Hank had no doubt. From what he'd seen, these two could squeeze information from petrified wood.

"Mr. D." Hank looked over at Henry and found his hand waving. He left Nick to check on his student, confident his date with Sadie would go off without a hitch.

HALLOWEEN

Saturday afternoon, Hank and Mickey picked up the kayaks from Mickey's storage unit. Jody and Nick had helped Mickey prepare their dinner, and Hank would text Mickey when they were thirty minutes out so he'd know when to deliver it.

Hank arrived at the farm right after lunch, the air balmy, the sky so impossibly blue it hurt his eyes. Somehow he found a space to park in front of the deli next to a big sign announcing gardening classes led by none other than Jody Claws. Hank hid the smile that threatened. Jody and Nick had more hidden talents than anyone he knew.

He climbed the steps to the deli, the neon sign in the front window flashing open. Pushing inside, he weaved through the cluster of customers, searching for Sadie, but couldn't find her.

They'd agreed to meet here, but he was early. He went back outside, following the sound of Jody's voice. She had a group of seven women and three men on their knees digging in soil so dark, it made him think of the black granite mined in northeast Vermont.

She glanced up, saw Hank, and waved him over. "Are you looking for Sadie?"

"Yes, have you seen her?"

She pointed down the path that led to the two-story house at the far end of the property.

Hank thanked her and followed the walkway to the house. He went up the steps and knocked on the door.

"Just a minute," Sadie called out. A moment later, the door swung open and Sweet Pea rushed at him. Hank squatted and rubbed her ears as he gazed up to find Sadie's vibrant green eyes assessing him. "What are you doing here?" she asked.

"Jody told me I'd find you here."

Her expression became guarded. "How did she know where I was?"

He rose and leaned against the doorjamb, a slow grin lifting his lips. "If you haven't realized it yet, Jody and Nick are tracking our every move because they're playing matchmaker."

"You'd have to be blind, deaf, and dumb to not have figured that out." She grabbed her purse, gave Sweet Pea a pat goodbye, then pulled the door shut.

Hank escorted her down the steps and up the path to his truck. "You look fantastic." That trim body tucked into shorts and tank top, brown hair pulled into a ponytail, and her wide smile made him want to scoop her into his arms and kiss her.

She cast a sidelong gaze at him, a smile tugging the corners of her mouth. "Is that a polite way of telling me I clean up good?"

Hank blinked away the thoughts. "Absolutely not. That was a compliment, no strings attached." He took her hand and slowly twirled her in a circle, his gaze sweeping over her. "You always look fabulous."

Her cheeks turned as rosy as the holly berries growing along the fence.

Interesting. He hadn't expected such an intense reaction. Did his opinion matter that much to her? "I don't give halfhearted compliments. What I say comes from the heart."

Sadie's throat worked, but no words came forth. Finally, she swallowed and said, "You are not at all what I thought you were the first time we met."

"I think we both made assumptions without getting the facts." He slid his hand under her elbow and started walking again. "We need to get moving if we're going to float the river and have our picnic before dark."

"The river?"

Hank cast a quick glance at her. "Yeah. According to Jody and Nick, you enjoy kayaking, so I borrowed Mickey's kayaks. The plan is to paddle down the river and have a picnic dinner at Drake Park. Were they wrong?"

Sadie gaped at him, then shook her head. "No, I love kayaking. I just don't get much time for it."

Hank picked up his pace, going in the opposite direction of Jody to avoid using precious time chit-chatting. Sadie followed without a word of complaint obviously thinking the same thing, or she wanted to avoid further matchmaking attempts. For some reason, the idea bothered him.

They reached his truck, and he helped her into the passenger side, then slid into the driver's seat. Twenty minutes later, they were in the kayaks and ready to take off.

Sadie placed her phone in the airtight compartment, then pushed her kayak into the water and climbed in.

His gaze tracked her from the sparkle in her eyes to the perfectly sculpted backside that left him wanting a whole lot more than just a trip down the river.

CHAPTER 12

They glided downriver, the afternoon sun warm overhead just as the weather forecaster had promised. The section Hank chose had a slow, meandering current that gave them time to talk while they floated.

"How about we use this time to get to know more about each other?"

Sadie watched a flock of geese take flight, then angled her face toward him. "I'd like that."

"Tell me how you got into farming."

Sadie released a sigh that sounded a lot like contentment. "My parents had an old house on the upper westside with a double lot, and my father loved gardening. From my earliest memory, I helped him weed and plant." She paused, then said, "They died in a car accident just before my sixteenth birthday."

"I'm sorry. I can't imagine losing both parents at the same time," Hank said.

"It was incredibly hard." She paused, blinking rapidly as she stared at a pair of otters frolicking on the beach. "They were the only family I had. My foster parents were kind, but it just wasn't the same."

"Are you still in contact with them?"

"Yes, we've stayed in touch, but I only lived with them a year. I graduated high school early, then left for college. I needed to get away from all the memories, and I needed a fresh start." Sadness momentarily pinched her expression then it was gone. "When I went to college, I majored in horticulture with a minor in entomology."

Rather than press her for more details, he let her set the pace. "So you're a bug and plant lady."

Her soft laughter stirred something inside of him he'd thought had died after Lydia's betrayal.

"I like that. After graduation, they offered me a teaching and research position in the entomology department at the University of Snowside." Her expression wavered a moment before she continued. "I rented the house from Elroy. Back then it was on a weed-filled eyesore. I asked if he'd mind if I planted a garden." Her smile was infectious. "I don't think he realized just how big a *garden* I had in mind."

"Knowing Elroy, I doubt he cared."

Her eyes warmed with fondness. "He didn't, and I think as the *garden* grew and grew, the results pleased him since the weeds were gone, along with the trash that accumulated because it had become a dumping ground. Turned out it was a win-win for both of us."

"When did you go into full-time farming?" Hank asked.

"It was a gradual transition. I was teaching at the university, and I kept proposing nonchemical research, and kept getting rejected."

"That surprises me with the push for organic and/or sustainable farming."

"That was a decade ago, and things have changed a lot since those days. Honestly, it was Elroy who pushed me to leave my job, a secure job with benefits and retirement, and farm the land.

I'm so glad he did. It's been tough, but I'm finally seeing some success." She looked over at him. "Enough about me. What about you?"

"I'm sure Elroy's already filled you in."

"Just a brief sketch, but no details."

Hank snorted. "That sounds like him. Just enough to whet your appetite, but no more."

Again, Sadie nodded. "That's about the size of it. I'll let you fill in the rest."

Hank didn't miss the impish grin that tilted her lips. She enjoyed putting him in the hot seat. "Where do you want me to start?"

"How about your time in the military?"

Hank dipped his paddle in the water. "As you know, Mickey and I served together—two tours in Afghanistan. He was tougher than me. He went back a third, but I couldn't do it."

"Understandable."

"When I left the military, I had offers for security work, and some government jobs along that same line, but I needed a fresh start, so I went back to school. The problem was, I didn't know what I wanted to do. I kept thinking about all the children we'd seen in Afghanistan, especially the girls denied an education, and an idea formed—teaching. I wanted to do something worthwhile, and what better way than to help mold and shape the next generation? It was so totally different from being a SEAL, and it appealed to me on a deep, visceral level. It sounds overly dramatic, but that's how it happened."

Sadie dipped her oar in the water to keep her kayak on course. "It doesn't sound that way at all. It sounds like you found your calling."

Hank studied the river as a beaver slapped the water. "Yes, I suppose you're right."

"How did you decide on kindergartners?"

"I couldn't decide what age group I wanted to teach. One of my professors suggested I volunteer in different classrooms and age groups to figure out which appealed to me. I started with high school, assuming I'd connect there. Ha! I'd rather face down the Taliban single-handedly. Those kids chewed me up and spit me out. I tried middle school next. A fun age, and I enjoyed them, but it just didn't feel like the right fit. I checked out preschool, but that wasn't for me, either. Finally, I went to kindergarten, and the minute I walked in the door, I knew that was where I belonged."

"It's funny how some things in life just hit like a bolt of lightning, isn't it?"

"It is," he said.

A light breeze ruffled Sadie's hair as they paddled along in silence, and Hank stilled the urge to run his fingers through her hair.

Inhaling a deep breath, Sadie smiled as a pair ducks floated alongside her kayak. "It's so peaceful here without the constant hum of traffic and crowds of people. Not that I don't love my customers and the hustle and bustle of the city, but I can't really avoid it with the farm smack dab in the middle of it all. Still, it's nice to have quiet time on the water with good company."

Fingers of late afternoon sunshine slanted through the cluster of maple trees lining the banks, their leaves a brilliant red as Hank and Sadie paddled into the Drake Park. Pulling the kayaks onto the sandy shore, Sadie's eyes widened when she saw a nearby picnic table covered with a crisp, white tablecloth set for two.

"You've been busy."

"I had a little help."

"Clearly."

Hank escorted her over to the table. "You told me how you got into farming, but the thing I'm really curious about is why you're still single."

Silence, broken only by the squawk of a pair of black birds fighting over a chunk of bread.

Just when he thought she wouldn't respond, she said, "I was married once—briefly."

Surprise etched Hank's features. He hadn't expected that. "What were you, a teenager?"

Sadie laughed. "No, it was my last year of college, and one of those decisions that seemed like a good idea at the time. We got along well. We had a lot in common, but once we got married, it all fell apart."

"Do you still see him?"

Sadie shook her head. "He moved away not long after we divorced. He's remarried with a couple of kids."

For some reason, the fact that he had a family sent relief coursing through Hank. The possibility that Sadie might yearn for her ex bothered him.

Like you yearn for Lydia?

Maybe it was time to bury the past and move on.

"This is delicious." Sadie sampled the simple fare again. "What restaurant is it from?"

Hank grinned. "From the kitchen of Mickey with help from Jody and Nick. The man is a pretty decent cook, so long as he's not trying a new recipe."

Sadie's mouth sagged. "Seriously?"

"Yes."

"Wow. I'm amazed he's still single. He cooks and styles hair —every woman's dream man."

Amused at the analogy, Hank chuckled. "I'd never looked at it that way. He has no end of women chasing after him, so that must be the reason."

"Maybe, but Annie told me she thinks he's avoiding serious attachments."

Hank considered her comment and realized she was probably right. "That makes sense. I think it still might be a hangover from his stint in the Middle East. Some scars take a lot of time to heal."

"I can certainly understand that."

The compassion in her expression moved him deeply. Maybe this was a woman he could open up to, bare his deepest, innermost feelings, something he'd never been comfortable doing with Lydia.

Her thigh pressed against his as her lips parted. Following his heart, he dipped his head and pressed his lips to hers. She tasted sweeter than the richest dessert.

When she didn't resist, he curled an arm around her and drew her closer, deepening the kiss. Her breasts cradled against his chest and sent his pulse into the stratosphere.

He pulled back, his breathing erratic.

She leaned her forehead against his. "That was unexpected."

Did she mean the kiss or something more?

"Good or bad, unexpected?" he murmured into her ear.

Her breath whispered over him. "Definitely good."

CHAPTER 13

November

A cold, wet nose pressed against Sadie's cheek the next morning. Cracking open an eye, she found a furry chin resting on the bed beside her. This *was not* the face she'd been dreaming about. The face in her dreams had intense blue eyes, twin dimples, and a rugged jaw that made her breath catch in anticipation.

But instead of Hank, Sweet Pea stared up at her. "It's Sunday," she grumbled, but Sweet Pea only panted in response. One day was the same as the next to her. It didn't matter it was Sunday and technically Sadie's only day off.

She peered at the clock.

Seven.

At least she'd waited rather than her usual five o'clock wake up call.

Stretching, Sadie rolled out of bed and went down to make coffee, her thoughts still on her dreams of Hank.

The more time she spent with him, the more she wanted to spend with him—exactly how it had been with Luke.

The thought gave her pause. Maybe she needed to take a breath and a step back before she drove Hank away like she'd done Luke.

Pushing thoughts of Hank aside, she carried her coffee to the porch to enjoy the semi-quiet morning. Sundays meant significantly less traffic, as most people weren't out and about until after ten.

What would it be like to actually live in the country versus carving out her little piece of farmland in the middle of a bustling metropolis? As tempting as it was at times, she enjoyed having the best of both. Farming in the hub of activity offered people the opportunity to see agriculture up close and personal without leaving the city.

There were the other farms in the city, but they didn't farm full-time, which was why she enjoyed her occasional outing to Old Time Christmas Tree Farm. It gave her an opportunity to chat and compare notes with Jeremy and Marilyn about farming. They understood the challenges she faced, and if not for them, she'd be totally alone in this enterprise.

Jeremy had been pressing her to expand and hire additional help and warned if she didn't, she'd burn out. He was right of course, but the problem came down to money. Her five-year plan contained big dreams that seemed silly and unattainable in her current position.

Sweet Pea sighed and laid her chin on Sadie's thigh. The dog read her moods better than she did herself. She stroked the silky fur. "I'm okay. I just get a little down when things don't go as expected."

Copper-flecked brown eyes stared up at her, and Sadie fought the urge to bury her face in Sweet Pea's soft fur and cry out her frustration. Instead, she smiled. "It's all going to work out. Just wait and see."

Her cell phone rang, interrupting the moment. She glanced at the screen and saw it was Annie. She swiped it and said, "Hey you, what's up?"

"Not much. Same old, same old. We're going to brunch and were hoping you'd join us."

"Oh my gosh, I would love to. What time?"

"Nine-thirtyish. Will that give you enough time to get ready?"

"Plenty of time. Where are we meeting?" Sadie asked. The last time she'd seen Annie, Jack, and Zoe was the fundraiser at Job Hunters 4 You. She suspected the invitation had more to do with her date last night, but she didn't care if that's what motivated the invitation. She'd endure Annie's grilling if it meant spending time with her three favorite people.

"I reserved a table at On the Pier with a view of the river."

"My favorite place. I've missed you guys."

"We've missed you, too."

"I'll see you there." Sadie went inside to shower and dress, a skip in her step.

Sweet Pea danced at her feet, sensing her change in mood, the Christmas bells Jody attached to her collar jingling. Even the reminder of the upcoming holidays didn't dampen Sadie's mood.

THE HOSTESS GUIDED Sadie through the dining room decorated to the hilt for the holidays. A massive Christmas tree in the far corner, tables decked out with deep green tablecloths and sprigs of holly in vases. Obviously, Jody was right. Everyone but Sadie got into the holiday spirit early.

Annie, Jack, Mickey, and Zoe had a table looking over the water, Christmas lights circling the huge picture window that faced the marina. Frost dotted the boats moored on the water, the weather making a complete one-eighty from yesterday's balmy mid-seventies.

Annie jumped up and hugged her when she reached the table, then Zoe cried out from her booster seat, "Aunt Sadie!"

Sadie scooped the little girl into her arms for a slobbery kiss and hugs. "How you doing, kiddo?"

Zoe's lopsided grin sent Sadie's biological clock tick-tocking into overdrive. "Good. How come you haven't come seen me?" the little girl demanded.

Sadie settled into the chair next to Annie, Zoe on her lap. "I've been working."

"Mommy says you're a *workerholic*."

Sadie ruffled her curls, shooting a glance at Annie, who only shrugged and mouthed, "I'm not wrong."

The waitress brought menus. "Will anyone else be joining you?"

"Yes, two more," Annie said.

"Can I bring coffee while you're waiting?"

"Yes, please," Jack said, clearly in need of a boost of caffeine, but Sadie fixed her attention on Annie.

Something in her tone sent her radar up. "Who else is coming?"

Mickey's brows drew together. "Yes, who else?"

Before Annie could respond, Zoe broke in, demanding hot chocolate. By the time the waitress left, Hank stood at Sadie's elbow.

Sadie cast a sidelong glance at Annie, who had the grace to blush at her blatant attempt at playing Cupid.

He shook hands with Mickey and Jack, but his gaze rested on Sadie the entire time, doing funny things to her insides.

Taking the chair next to hers, Zoe studied him as if were one of the lizards on the farm that fascinated her. "Mommy says you're Aunt Sadie's boyfriend."

Heat raced across Sadie's cheeks. Out of the mouth of babes. She'd have to talk with Annie about what she said in front of the preschooler.

Hank took her comment in stride. "Well, I hope I'm her friend, and I'm definitely a boy, so I'm guessing you're right."

Zoe turned her intent gaze on Sadie. "Is he your friend, Aunt Sadie?"

Sadie continued to stare into Hank's eyes, trying to decipher his thoughts, but his blank expression gave away nothing. "Yes, we're friends."

"Good. Help me color."

Question answered. Time to move on.

Sadie heaved a sigh when Zoe dropped the subject, but one look at Annie told her she'd be revisiting the topic. Fortunately, the waitress arrived with their coffee.

"I want to color," Zoe said, her tone turning strident.

Mickey shoved the paper and crayons across the table and she concentrated on choosing a crayon from the box.

"So, who else are we waiting for?" Mickey asked.

Sadie caught a flash of mischief in Annie's expression.

"Oh, just a friend," Annie said, with a negligent wave of her hand.

"Who?" he persisted.

Annie's evasiveness had Sadie's curiosity up. Who was the mysterious sixth person?

"Annieeeeeee."

Annie pushed back from the table as her neighbor, Sarah Barker, rushed up, flinging her arms around her. "Thank you so much for inviting me. It's been forever," she said, hugging her tight.

"I know. We live next door and never see each other."

Sadie rose, blocking Mickey from Sarah's view. Annie was most definitely playing matchmaker with Mickey and Sarah and her and Hank. Hoping to ward off the dustup in the making, Sadie smiled at Sarah.

"Sadieeeeeee," she cried out, squeezing her tight. "I don't remember the last time I saw you."

Sadie hadn't seen her in months. Sarah's workload as a guidance counselor at Snowside High allowed for little free time.

"How are you?" Sadie asked.

"Crazy busy. It's always this way as we head into the holidays."

"What about you? How's the farm going?"

Sadie launched into the news about the farm, her new volunteer, and Hank's class tour. Finally, she'd stalled as long as she could and sat down, waiting for the fireworks to erupt. She wasn't disappointed.

Sarah stared across the table at Mickey. Their eyes met, a collective silence falling over the group.

Finally, Annie said, "Why don't you take the seat beside Hank?"

Sarah stood rooted in place. Taking the seat by Hank meant she'd be sitting next to Mickey, which Sadie was certain she didn't want to do. Mickey and Sarah had been on a couple of dates Annie told her, then something had happened that both refused to discuss. And no matter how hard Annie pried, Sarah had refused to tell her.

The scathing expression she shot Annie said it all. She'd rather walk on hot coals than sit next to Mickey, but rather than make a scene, she sat down.

Hank leaned in and whispered in her ear. "Wonder how Mickey likes the shoe being on the other foot?"

Sadie pressed her lips together to still the laugher building inside her. "From his expression, I'd say he's not enjoying it."

Hank's eyes crinkled with barely suppressed merriment. "The understatement of the year."

Suddenly, Sadie was very glad they weren't enemies anymore.

CHAPTER 14

After brunch, Hank joined Mickey for their Sunday afternoon pickup game of basketball. By the time they finished, sweat drenched Hank's body. They drove to a nearby pub for beer and burgers. Once they placed an order at the bar, they found a table where they could watch the game.

"So, from the way you and Sadie cozied up at brunch, it looks like your date went well last night," Mickey said.

Hank expected an interrogation, and frankly, he'd thought Mickey would press him while they played since he'd been a pivotal player in bringing the date together. But doing so meant Mickey would be in the hot seat, too, because Hank wanted to know what was going on between him and Sarah.

"It did, in a large part, thanks to your help," he said, tapping his beer to Mickey's.

Hank studied Mickey, appreciating their friendship and support. He hadn't realized how he'd missed the camaraderie of his fellow SEALs. But he had. That might've been why he'd had a difficult time living in Angel Falls. He really hadn't found the support and friendship like he had here.

"When are you seeing her again?" Mickey asked.

Hank took another pull of his beer. "We didn't make plans." He wasn't about to tell him he was thinking of going to see her tomorrow after school.

Mickey rolled his eyes. "What are you waiting for? Clearly she's into you."

Hank sipped his beer before responding. "I could say the same about you and Sarah."

Silence.

"We aren't talking about my love life," Mickey said at last.

"Why not?"

Mickey shifted in his chair, his usually direct gaze staring off into the distance. "I don't want to talk about Sarah."

A charged silence followed, broken only by a heated argument at the next table over a call made by the referee, telling Hank he'd touched a nerve.

"What's going on? I thought you two were getting along?" Hank munched on a pretzel as he waited for Mickey's response.

"We had a little misunderstanding," Mickey hedged.

"What kind of misunderstanding?"

Mickey waved a hand, dismissing the incident. "It was nothing. It'll blow over. I'm just giving her some time to cool off."

"Exactly how long has it been?"

Mickey shrugged. "A few weeks."

"Weeks! You need to talk to her."

Mickey shook his head. "I told you, I'm giving her space."

"Space for what?" Hank asked. "You need to talk to her. This is the stuff that gets worse, not better when you stay silent."

Defiance lit Mickey's eyes. "She could call me, too."

Hank stared at him until he squirmed. "True, but are you willing to risk never seeing her again? You need to call her, or better yet, go see her."

Mickey was silent a long moment, then said, "Time to change the subject."

Hank hoped he'd call her because he thought they'd make a perfect couple.

HANK WENT to Sadie's after he left the school the next afternoon. He didn't know what the dating protocol was, but he couldn't wait to see her again. He'd enjoyed her company, so why not see if she felt the same?

Twinkling Christmas lights ran the length of the porch, around the pillars, front window, and the bushes lining the walkway. A Santa and sleigh with eight reindeer filled the yard, Rudolph's nose flashing red.

Jody hadn't wasted any time getting the Halloween decorations down and Christmas decorations up.

Hank went inside to find Jody behind the makeshift desk she'd set up. She smiled and waved at him.

Prancer slept curled into Sweet Pea and neither animal raised their head at Hank's arrival. "What are you doing here?" Jody asked.

The sparkle in her eyes told him it was more than casual interest. Mickey had warned him she had a vested interest in bringing him and Sadie together. A matchmaking Mrs. Claus interfering in his budding relationship with Sadie had trouble written all over it.

"I just dropped by to see Sadie," he said. "Is she out in the field?"

"Actually, she's in the back sorting vegetables." Jody gestured behind her. "Take the hallway to the end and turn right. You can't miss her."

Hank thanked her and headed down the hallway before she could voice more questions. He entered the back room and found Sadie busily sorting vegetables. "Need any help?"

She glanced up, her smile warm and welcoming. "Hey, stranger. I didn't expect to see you today."

He moved closer, returning her smile. "I've been wanting to see you, so I thought I'd stop by, give you a hand, and spend time with you. A win/win, so to speak."

She brushed the dirt from her hands and hugged him. "I'm glad you did."

Hank's arm tightened around her before she could slip away. His gaze fell on her parted lips. His hand slid to the back of her head and he slowly lowered until his lips touched hers.

Sadie's eyes widened in surprise, an instant before she melted against him, her arms twining around his neck.

When he eased back, she fanned her face. "That was—amazing." Her voice slightly breathless, she said, "I'm so glad you stopped by because I wanted to tell you again what a great time I had on Saturday."

Hank leaned in, brushing his nose against hers. "I'm glad," he said, his voice rough with emotion. He gestured to the table where Sadie worked. "What are you doing?"

"Making CSA baskets for tomorrow's deliveries."

"CSA?"

"Community Sponsored Agriculture. We have customers who pay a membership fee to have vegetables delivered weekly."

Hank nodded in understanding as he rolled up his sleeves. "What can I do to help?"

Sadie showed how to separate the vegetables into boxes. As they worked, she asked about his class. "How are the kids doing?"

"Would you believe they're already getting hyped about Thanksgiving and Halloween was Saturday?"

"I believe it. Halloween is the kickoff to the holiday season, or so Jody keeps telling me."

"Jody would know. She and Nick really get into the Christmas spirit."

"They do."

Hank studied her less than exuberant expression. "But you don't feel the same way?"

Sadie focused on sorting the vegetables. "I'm not a kid."

"Neither am I, but I love the holidays, spending time with my family." He leaned toward her with a conspiratorial whisper. "Who doesn't love getting and giving presents?"

Her silence surprised him.

He touched her arm. "What's wrong?"

She set the basket aside and met his questioning gaze. "I don't celebrate the holidays."

"For religious reasons?"

Sadie shook her head. "It's just not my thing."

Hank didn't believe that was the real reason. Who wouldn't love receiving a little surprise, even if it was a box of chocolate, or flowers, or bath salts?

She started another basket. "So, how's Elroy?"

Obviously, she wanted a change of subject and he would—for now—but eventually he would insist on the truth. His mother's words came back to give him a private laugh.

I believe in honesty, except when it's directed at me.

Hank finished off a basket as he filled her in on Elroy, then asked, "Do you usually do this by yourself?"

Sadie paused, taken aback by his question. The men she'd dated since her divorce had little interest in her work. Hank stood out as the exception to them.

"Usually, Milly comes in to help, but she couldn't make it today. I really need two full-time workers."

"I get it. Managing my students with just one aide is a real challenge. Nick has been a tremendous help, but I can't imagine doing this all on your own." He made a sweeping gesture to include the farm.

Sadie collected the filled baskets and moved them to another table, then set another box of vegetables on the table. "I can't imagine handling twenty-five kids all by yourself, especially that age group."

"It's difficult," Hank admitted. "Even with Rosario, who is amazing, the kids need more attention than just two adults can give them. And Kristin needs extra help."

"I thought the state provided extra assistance for disabled students?"

"They do, but it's difficult to find an aide who's qualified, plus the school district doesn't pay them enough, so the ones that are really good go to school districts that offer better pay."

"I can certainly understand that. If you don't mind me asking, it seems like a lot of your students are struggling financially. Am I wrong?"

"No, you're not. Many are struggling and housing is a real concern. There just isn't enough affordable housing."

"I've been really concerned about the housing shortage in Snowside."

"Me, too. I've tried petitioning the city council to take action, but I've gotten nowhere," Hank said.

"It's frustrating, isn't it?"

"It is."

Sadie placed a bundle of beets into the basket. "I was at a conference in New Hampshire a few years ago, and I toured a farm that created a community, or as they called it a present-day village with an emphasis on bringing people together around agriculture. They converted old barns into retail stores and restaurants, and the farm had its own restaurant that used produce from the farm, a community garden, and surrounding it were condominiums designed for families and singles—everything interconnected with the farm. It was amazing. I would love to have my farm be part of something like that."

"Wouldn't housing be expensive?" Hank asked.

"I don't know what it cost, but if I were doing it, I'd want to have a mix of homeowners from people on fixed incomes, low-income families—generational housing—that's community, not just housing slapped up where people move on after a few years. I want a place where people want to stay—not a stepping stone to move on."

"Are you considering something like that here?" Hank said.

Sadie snorted. "Hardly. It's a pipedream and where would I put the housing? And not to mention the fact that I keep getting turned down for loans to buy this land."

Hank said nothing, and she couldn't gage his reaction. Finally, he asked, "What about the property adjacent to this with all the old buildings? It would be the perfect place."

She'd considered it several times, especially since it would triple the land she had now. "It would, but there's no way I could finance it."

They finished the baskets, and Sadie carried them into the walk-in cooler, setting them on the shelves for delivery first thing in the morning. Closing the door, she turned to find Hank beside her. She tilted her head to look into his eyes and really liked what she saw. Chiseled cheeks, square jaw, nicely spaced eyes filled with kindness, compassion, and humor. And those lips! When they'd touched hers earlier… Her breath stalled at the memory.

Pulling herself together, she said, "I can't tell you how much I appreciate the help. I finished twice as fast, and it didn't feel like work."

His fingers stroked the hair away from her face, his eyes locking with hers. His voice a soft whisper of sound, he said, "It didn't feel like work to me, either."

He leaned in and brushed his lips over hers. Sadie's eyes

drifted closed as she leaned into him, inhaling his scent, his taste. She wanted more and pressed her body tighter to his.

A throat cleared. "Sorry to interrupt," Jody said. "I just wanted you to know I was leaving."

Sadie turned to face Jody, her back pressed against Hank's chest. "Thank you so much. I know movie night is going to be amazing because of your hard work."

She hugged Jody, then pulled back to find the older woman grinning. "This is what I live for, and tomorrow I've got some new ideas I want to share with you. Right now, I'll leave you two and head home to Nicky."

Sadie waved goodbye and once they were alone, she turned back to Hank. "I'm making spaghetti if you don't have other plans." Her pulse accelerated as she waited for his answer, and it surprised her how much she wanted him to spend the evening with her.

Hank's grin was infectious. "The only plan I had was a TV dinner in front of the game—alone."

"Then how about beer, spaghetti with meatballs, French bread, salad fresh from the farm, and Monday night football with me?"

"That's the best offer I've had all day."

Sadie whistled for Sweet Pea, then crooked a finger at Hank. "Follow me."

CHAPTER 15

Hank was glad he hadn't waited until the weekend to see Sadie again. Working with her had been pure joy, and he'd had more fun than he'd expected. How he'd thought she was anything like Lydia, he didn't know. One thing Hank knew with certainty, the more time he spent with her, the more time he wanted to spend with her.

Sadie turned on the football game and got them each a beer while they worked together in the kitchen, watching Buffalo and the Jets battle it out. Sadie was a diehard Buffalo fan, while Hank lived and died with the Jets.

"So what makes you a Buffalo fan?" Hank asked.

"I just like rooting for the underdog," Sadie said, "but, of course, this year they're doing much better. What about you? Why the Jets?"

"My dad. When I was growing up, he was a rabid Jets fan. I remember my brother told him he was rooting for the Giants once when we were kids, and I thought my dad would blow a gasket. He only did it to annoy Dad, and it worked."

"Your dad sounds like an interesting guy."

"He was. He's been gone ten years, and I still miss him."

Sadie's eyes darkened with sympathy. "I'm sorry."

"It's hard losing a parent."

Sadie stirred the sauce. "It is. If you don't mind my asking, what happened?"

His tone brisk, he said, "Heart attack." Taking a slow inhale, the tension drained from his body. "Dad was fifty when he died. A virus attacked his heart, and he was on a waiting list for a transplant, but he died before he got one."

Sadie covered his hand with hers, giving it a gentle squeeze. "I'm so sorry. It must have been really difficult for you and your family."

"Yeah, losing Dad was tough." Hank momentarily got sucked into those dark days, but he shook it off and said, "What happened to your parents?"

Her voice took on an empty hollowness he hadn't heard before. "They hit a patch of ice on their way home, spun out of control, and went head on into a semi-truck."

Their eyes met and held. His fingers threaded through hers. "I'm sorry."

Her voice barely audible, she whispered. "Thank you." Clearing her throat, she stepped away and put the noodles into the boiling water, then handed Hank the pasta server to stir them while she prepared the salad.

Changing the subject, she asked, "You said you were in the military and did two tours in Afghanistan with Mickey, is that right?"

Hank studied her for a long moment and considered pressing her for details on her parents, but let it drop for now. "Yes," he said.

Her gaze flickered over him. "I'm sorry. Are my questions too personal? I only ask because I'd like to get to know you better."

Hank flashed back to those years in Afghanistan. While Mickey avoided talking about it, the silence only made it worse.

Hank chose the opposite tack. "It's okay. I don't talk about it a lot. Only with people I know and trust."

Something shimmered in her eyes he couldn't define. "Do you trust me?" she asked.

Hank's fingers caressed her cheek before he pressed his lips to hers. He pulled back and said, "I do."

She smiled at him. "You can tell me anything. No matter how difficult."

Hank believed her. "We were just kids when we signed up. I was twenty-two, and Mickey was twenty-three. We thought we were going to see the world."

"And did you?"

"We did, but not how we expected. Our first deployment, we were sent to Germany and then to the Ukraine, but we saw little of the country. Our next assignment was Afghanistan. Some ruggedly beautiful country, but a lot of poverty and suffering. We didn't effect much change while we were there, either."

"I'm sorry," Sadie said, her fingers tracing the line of his jaw.

Hank took her hand and kissed her fingertips.

She pressed her body against his, and he slipped his arms around her, holding her close. He pressed his nose into her hair and inhaled. Her scent filled him, and her warmth seeped into him, taking away the pain of the past.

He lowered his head and kissed her again, a gentle press of lips.

She sighed, and he deepened the kiss, her fingers running through his hair.

"Oh my," she said, when they broke off the kiss.

Oh, my indeed.

THEY ATE dinner in front of the TV. Afterward, Hank insisted she sit while he did the dishes, and she agreed mainly because that kiss they'd shared before dinner had rocked her to her core. She needed some distance from him before she hauled him to her bedroom and did a whole lot more than kiss. And she wasn't ready for that—yet.

Sadie found it an incredible turn-on as he rinsed and loaded the dishwasher, his forearms flexing as he worked. Strong hands wiped the counters and put the food away. All the while, she wanted those hands on her body.

He looked up once and caught her staring. Their eyes held for long moments. Finally, she blinked and looked away, but he'd rattled her. She wanted him more than she'd ever wanted a man.

He dried his hands and hung the dish towel, then finished the last swig of his beer. "Thanks for dinner. It was great. Next time I cook."

Sadie managed a shaky smile and pushed to her feet, her legs rubbery. "I'd love that."

"I need to get home and work on my lesson plan for tomorrow."

Sadie, with Sweet Pea at her heels, walked him to his truck as snow drifted from the sky. "I can't tell you how much I appreciate your help today."

She raised up on tiptoe, slipping her arms around his neck, and pressed her lips to his.

His arm came around her waist and lifted her until her feet came off the ground as he deepened the kiss. When he pulled back, they were both breathing heavily.

Sadie leaned her forehead to his, willing her body to return to its slow, steady breathing.

His cheek brushed hers as he whispered, "You set me on fire. Whenever I'm with you, I can't think straight."

"You do the same thing to me."

Sweet Pea worked her way between them and released a low whine. Hank laughed and rubbed her ears, then opened his truck door, climbed inside, and rolled down the window. Bracing an arm on the frame, he said, "I'll pick you up Saturday for dinner at my place."

Happiness radiated from deep inside her. "I can't wait." She leaned in, pressed a quick kiss to his lips, knowing that with anything more they'd end up in her bed.

Instead, she waved as he drove away, happier than she'd been in a long, long time.

CHAPTER 16

Elroy dropped by the farm two days later at closing. He went inside the deli to the back room where Jody had told him to meet her and Nick.

He found the two huddled at her desk, Prancer and Sweet Pea sleeping on the floor at their feet. Sweet Pea cracked open an eye and wagged her tail in greeting.

Elroy bent to pat her and Prancer, then took the only other seat.

Jody handed him a steaming cup of hot chocolate and pushed a platter of Christmas star cookies toward him. He took one and settled back in his seat, studying his two cohorts. "Well, I hope this meeting means that you two have made progress."

Nick's bellowing laughter filled the room. "When have you not known us to make progress?"

Elroy chewed his cookie and studied the two thoughtfully. "Never. All your assignments have always been successful. I just don't want this to be your first failure."

Jody stiffened and huffed out a breath. "I don't think I take kindly to your insinuation I'm messing this up. We've never failed, and I have no intention of starting now. And let's not forget the farm tour was a huge success."

Elroy held up a hand to placate her. "I'm sorry. I didn't mean any disrespect, and you're right. The farm tour made Sadie see that Hank really is a nice guy. I'm just nervous because I want to see my nephew and Sadie happy. And I think the only way to accomplish that is to bring them together."

Jody relaxed back in her chair. "And we want the same thing. I think we've made some good progress, but I won't deny we still have a long way to go."

"So, what's the next move?" Elroy asked.

"That's why we asked you here so we can brainstorm."

"What are our options?" Elroy asked.

Jody's gaze slid to Nick's, and it was as if a telepathic connection passed between them. "I've got a couple of ideas, but we're going to need your help to pull it off—if you're willing."

Elroy's gaze moved between the two as he tried to gauge exactly what their plan was. "You know I'll help in any way I can. Just tell me what to do."

Jody drummed red and gold nails on the countertop. "The way I see it, we've taken them from adversaries to friends to dating, but we need to step it up if we're going to bring them together by Christmas. We need them to fall in love, and the best way to accomplish that is to throw them together more frequently. Hank needs to step up his game. He's been burned by love, but he hasn't given up on it, whereas I think Sadie has. She's devoted herself to the farm, her friends, and Sweet Pea. If you asked her how she envisions her future, it would be alone. We need to make her want for more than work."

"And where do I come into this?" Elroy asked.

"Sadie is holding back from living. We need you to encourage her to reach out and grasp life, and I'm not just talking about

Hank—I'm talking about reaching for all of her dreams. Can you do that?"

"Absolutely. I plan on having dinner with her tonight, and I've set up a meeting with our congresswoman to help her get the loan for the farm. This has been a big dream for her."

Jody nodded. "I agree."

Sweet Pea gave a bark of agreement. If she was on board, he had to be on the right track.

SADIE HEARD the greenhouse door open. She glanced up to find Elroy with Sweet Pea on his heels headed her way. She rose, brushed the dirt from her knees, and hugged him. "Where have you been keeping yourself?" she asked.

"I've had some projects going and finally wrapped them up, so I came by to check on you."

"I'm so glad you did. I was just finishing up for the day. Will you stay and have dinner?"

Elroy's smile set a cascade of wrinkles skating across his face. "I was hoping you'd ask."

Sadie slipped her arm through his. "Let's go up to the house, get something to drink, and I'll make dinner."

She began walking without waiting for his response. Sweet Pea jetted in front of them as they exited the greenhouse, and Elroy wrapped his scarf around his neck.

They reached the farmhouse, went inside, and hung up their coats, then Sadie led him back to the kitchen. "I have beer or I could make Irish coffee if you'd prefer something hot to drink?"

"Irish coffee sounds perfect," Elroy said, rubbing his hands together to warm them. "Winter is definitely on the way."

Sadie nodded in agreement as she started the coffee, then took the brown sugar and a bottle of Irish whiskey from the overhead cupboard.

Turning on the oven, she turned to Elroy. "How does chicken pot pie sound?"

He rubbed his belly. "Delicious. It's one of my favorite meals."

Sadie busied herself fixing their drinks and as soon as the oven reach three hundred and fifty degrees, she slid in the glass dish, then sat down next to Elroy and sipped her coffee.

"Tell me about the projects you've been working on."

Elroy wrapped his hands around the mug and said, "I'm not ready to talk about them just yet, but I want to discuss something else with you."

"What?"

"The land."

Sadie's heart stuttered. Had he decided to sell it to someone else? "What about it?"

"Have you had any luck getting a loan?"

Sadie shook her head. "They just turned me down—again. Why? Have you changed your mind about waiting for me to get funding?"

Elroy sipped his coffee. "No, nothing like that. I've been thinking that you should reconsider and let me carry the note."

Sadie studied his earnest expression. "I appreciate the offer, but I can't do that. I don't want to tie up your money, and I don't want to give the appearance that I'm taking advantage of you, especially now that I'm dating Hank.""This is between you and me. Hank doesn't need to know about it."

"No, absolutely not. I won't keep this from him."

Elroy held up a hand in apology. "Okay, I get that. I have another idea."

Sadie eyed him suspiciously. "I'm listening."

"Didn't you tell me the loan keeps getting rejected because

you're zoned residential and the city refused your request to rezone agricultural?"

"Yes and yes."

"I've been doing some research. I think you need to contact Congresswoman Sheila Menudo and ask for her help."

"What good would that do?"

"A lot. First, she's a woman. Second, she's extremely supportive of small farms, and organic farms, in particular. Third, she's been very vocal about promoting women in agriculture. She's young, idealistic, and driven to make change. She also has connections and clout that you don't have."

"I like this idea."

"Good, because you have an appointment with her on Friday morning."

"W-W-What! I'm not ready to meet her. I need to—"

Elroy cut her off. "Stop with the excuses. You've got a dream, and this is your time to chase it. Stop putting off until tomorrow because tomorrow may never come." He squeezed her hand. "I know it's scary, but you need to do this now while you have the opportunity."

Sadie stilled, fear churning inside her. Elroy was right. She always threw up excuses and hesitated to jump in. He'd pushed her to go into full-time farming when she'd dragged her feet. Left on her own, she'd have stalled until she was old and gray. And even though he'd sprung this on her, he was right.

"I'll make it work," she said at last.

The timer went off. She pushed to her feet, hugged him, and whispered, "Thank you. I do drag my feet with anything new."

He patted her hand. "Change is scary."

It was terrifying. She took their dinner from the oven. While it cooled, she set the table, then served the pie.

Elroy took a bite and proclaimed, "Delicious."

"Good. I wasn't sure how it would turn out."

Sadie bit her tongue when Elroy slipped a piece of crust to Sweet Pea.

"So, is it serious between you and Hank?"

Sadie choked on the bite she'd just taken. "Serious? We've only been on a couple of dates."

Elroy gave her a negligent shrug. "Why are you so shocked? Have you ever heard of love at first sight?"

"No, not a believer." She'd been down that road and look what it cost her.

Elroy took another bite and chewed thoughtfully. "Yes, I can see that. Too practical."

Sadie took offense to that. "What does that mean?"

"It means you believe in what you can see and touch."

"Is there something wrong with that?"

"No, but you can also miss out on the magic life has to offer."

Elroy's words stayed with her long after he'd gone home. Being practical didn't mean she missed out on anything. She had a good life and was *almost* perfectly content.

CHAPTER 17

A nnie's infectious smile greeted Sadie Friday morning when she climbed onto the downtown bus. It helped ease the tension that had been churning inside her since Elroy told her about the appointment with Congresswomen Menudo.

Sadie scanned her card, then handed Annie a bag of canned goods for her holiday giveaway box.

"Oh, thank you. What are you doing here?" Annie asked, surprise evident in her tone as she tucked the canned food into her donation box.

And why wouldn't she be surprised? Any other Friday, Sadie would be working.

"I've got an appointment downtown at nine." She took the seat directly opposite Annie so they could chat while she drove. "How are you feeling?"

Annie adjusted her Christmas hat. She'd started wearing it the day after Halloween. Sadie didn't get everyone's obsession with the holidays and wondered if they made a Grinch hat. She pushed aside the negative thoughts.

"Wonderful. Haven't had a bit of nausea, but I have to admit by the end of the day I'm exhausted."

Sadie would take nausea and exhaustion to have what Annie had. "The fatigue might have as much to do with keeping up with a three-year-old as the pregnancy."

"Good point."

A little girl with dark, curly hair bounced onto the bus and handed Annie two cans. "Mommie said these are for the give-away box." She leaned in, crinkling her nose, and said in a stage whisper, "They're yucky green beans."

"Thank you," she said, sharing a laugh with the girl's mother. Mother and daughter took a seat.

Sadie watched them, another wave of envy sweeping over her. When had her biological clock started ticking out of control?

The minute you met Hank.

Sadie quickly tossed out that notion. This had nothing to do with Hank.

"How are things with you?" Annie asked, shutting the doors and pulling away from the curb.

"Good, and Jody is as talented as you said."

"Tell me what she's done."

Sadie spent most of the ride filling her in on all the events Jody had lined up.

"Wow, they all sound amazing. We'll have to bring Zoe to the Christmas movie night."

"You should. Hank's class will be there, too."

Annie cast a sidelong glance at her. "Interesting. We'll be there for sure. How's it going with you and Hank?"

"Fine."

Annie arched a brow at her. "Fine, that's the best you can do?"

Fortunately, Sadie reached her stop, preventing Annie from grilling her further. She pressed a kiss to her cheek, left with a "see you later," and headed toward the chrome and glass building on her left.

Taking the elevator up to the fifteenth floor, she checked in with the receptionist, then took a seat. As she waited, all the negative possibilities swirled through her mind. She wanted desperately to believe that this would be the answer to her funding problems, but she knew it was a long shot.

Sadie blew out an anxious breath and did some yoga breathing to settle her mind.

She'd barely calmed her whirling thoughts when the receptionist called her name. Rising, she went toward the congresswoman's door, determined to hope for the best, and even if this didn't work out, she'd keep looking. She wasn't giving up!

Congresswoman Sheila Menudo, a tiny wisp of a woman, welcomed Sadie at the door with a firm handshake and a wide smile that oozed confidence. Her greeting eased the churning inside Sadie, and she returned her smile, following her into the office.

The congresswoman motioned to the sofa, and they sat side-by-side. "Coffee?" she asked, pulling her long dark hair into a ponytail.

Sadie nodded, too nervous to speak. Thankfully, the woman chatted away as if they were old friends while she poured their coffee, handing a cup and saucer to Sadie.

"I love your farm, especially your Wednesday night grief group."

Sadie stared, her jaw sagging. "You've been to the grief group?"

"Oh yes. I started coming about six months ago, after my mother died. It was such a difficult time for me, and this gathering has made all the difference for me."

"I'm so glad the group helped."

The congresswoman leaned forward, her gaze intent, her

expression animated. "What you do there is so much than more farming."

Sadie clutched her coffee cup. "Thank you. It means a lot to know what I'm doing helps people."

Sheila relaxed back into the cushions. "So, tell me why you're here."

Sadie eased her hold on her cup, liking the congresswoman more and more, particularly her directness. "I need your help. For over a year, I've been applying for funding through the agriculture department to purchase the farm, and I keep getting turned down. They tell me I'm zoned residential and reject my application."

"That makes no sense! You're a perfect fit. You're a woman. You operate an urban farm. You're organic. You check off every box. How many times have you applied?"

"Four times in the past eighteen months."

The congresswoman frowned. "This is the most frustrating part of my job—seeing how slow government is to respond to its citizens." She sighed, and her direct gaze held Sadie's. "What can I do to help?"

Sadie inhaled. This was it. Now was her chance to make her pitch. "I came here to ask you to petition the agriculture department on my behalf in your capacity as a congresswoman."

She thought over Sadie's request, nodding slowly. "I'm more than happy to try, but I don't want to mislead you. I'm a junior congresswoman from Vermont, and I don't know how much clout I have."

"Don't sell yourself short. From what I've seen on the news, you've accomplished a lot in the short time you've been in office. I believe this is only the beginning."

She gave Sadie a grateful smile. "Thank you. I'm glad to know my constituents feel I'm accomplishing something, and please call me Sheila."

"Sadie."

They smiled at one another.

Sadie sipped her coffee, then set the cup and saucer down. "I know you're busy, so I won't take up more of your time."

With a wave of her hand, Sheila said, "Nonsense. I have time, and I'd really like to hear about your plans for the farm."

Prepared for just such a question, Sadie laid out her business plan, showing the improvements she'd made with the hydroponic system. She told her about her plans for the future, and she even shared her fantasy of purchasing the adjacent property, thanks to Hank's suggestion.

Sheila scribbled notes and asked pertinent questions.

Finally, when Sadie wound down, Sheila set her pad on the side table. "Your vision is incredible. Even if you can accomplish half of what you've proposed, you will be a model for other urban farms across the country. Besides the loan, I have some ideas for grant money for the housing. I believe there's some school funding you could apply for to get more hands-on farming for kids. Let me have my staff look into this, and I'll get back to you with what they find out, but my top priority will be funding for the land. My aid will keep you apprised of any progress we make, and if you don't hear from her, call."

Sadie blinked back tears, her relief so profound. Whether or not the congresswoman managed to secure funding, she believed in her and that meant more than she could ever express.

"Thank you." Sadie rose, shaking her hand, and Sheila walked her to the door.

"We will get your funding," she said. "I want this to work, and I intend to make you the poster child for women in agriculture."

Sadie left the building, zipping her coat as the brisk wind cut through her. Even if the congresswoman got only one of those sources of income, it would be amazing. She floated to the bus stop, her feet barely touching the pavement.

CHAPTER 18

At noon the next day, Annie and Jody shooed Sadie away from the farm, telling her she was done for the day and to get ready for her date. A passing wave of guilt swept over her at leaving them to manage the farm and movie night, even though Mickey, Jack, and Nick were helping, too.

After being assured they had everything in hand, Sadie finally left alone, as Sweet Pea had abandoned her to stay with Prancer. A smile teased across her lips as she took the path to her house to get ready for another evening with Hank. Rather than dread his company, now she looked forward to spending time with him. The man had a sense of humor that drew her, but he was also kind and caring, not to mention the way his eyes darkened with barely restrained passion when he looked at her.

Sadie's heart pounded just thinking about it.

Waving a hand in front of her face to cool her burning cheeks, she pushed through the front door and climbed the stairs to her bedroom. After she washed off the dirt and sweat, she stepped out of the shower, then took her time applying her makeup. She chose her warmest sweater and snow pants since Hank had told her they'd be outdoors part of the time and the temperatures were predicted in the teens. She also brought a change of clothes for dinner.

The doorbell rang just minutes after she put the finishing touches on her hair. She descended the stairs and opened the door to find Hank on the other side also dressed in a parka, snow pants, and boots.

He stepped inside and closed the door. The heat of his gaze sent her pulse skittering out of control. His arms came around and he pressed her against the door as his head lowered to kiss her.

Yes, oh yes. This was what she'd been waiting for!

Her arms snaked around his neck, and she arched her body against his muscled chest. She wanted to haul him upstairs, but instead she eased her arms away.

Why was she behaving like a giddy teenager?

They'd only gone from enemies to friends less than a month ago. Way too soon to take it any further than kissing.

His fingers traced the line of her jaw. "Whenever I see you, I have to touch you."

Sadie understood and felt the same way. "Me, too, but don't we need to leave?" She took her coat from the hook and slipped it on. "Where are we going?" she asked.

He winked at her before escorting her out the door. "Old Time Christmas Tree Farm."

She climbed into Hank's truck, and he headed north. All he'd told her was to dress warmly and bring clothes for dinner, but little else.

"Tell me more about what we're doing," Sadie said.

Hank's expression turned guarded. "Sorry, it's a surprise, so I'm keeping my mouth shut."

"I told you I'm not a fan of surprises."

His eyes twinkled with suppressed merriment. "Then why don't you ask me questions and see if you can figure it out?"

Sadie laughed. "Challenge accepted. Is what I'm wearing going to keep me warm?"

His gaze swept over her as he considered her clothing. "Debatable, but I brought extra blankets and clothing just in case."

Sadie drummed her fingers on the console between them. "Hmmm. Does that mean we're going to be outdoors the entire time?"

"A fair part of the time."

"Will we be sitting or doing something active?"

Hank's lips twitched. "A little of both."

Sadie shook her finger at him. "You can be awfully tight-lipped. Did you know that?"

He smirked. "So I've been told."

Sadie debated her next question. "Are we going to be doing much walking?"

Hank turned on the blinker and merged onto the highway, heading north. "It's possible there could be a fair amount of that."

"Will I need my skis?"

"I've brought everything you're going to need."

Sadie considered her next question. "Are you planning on feeding me a snack since I'm going to be exerting so much energy? I'll need sustenance."

Hank released a sudden burst of laughter. "If there's one thing I've learned in the time we've been dating—food is a necessity."

"You've been paying attention."

"I have. Are you done grilling me?"

Sadie quirked her mouth, her nose twisting to one side. "I suppose it's enough for now. Why?"

"Just preparing myself for the next barrage of questions."

Sadie laughed. While she might not be a fan of surprises, she'd made an exception with Hank.

A CLOUDLESS BLUE sky shone overhead as Hank left city traffic behind. Crossing his fingers, he hoped he'd found something Sadie would enjoy after the long hours she'd been working.

They reached the turnoff for Old Time Christmas Trees, and he followed the narrow lane to the parking lot. He helped Sadie out of the truck and escorted her to the entrance of the lot.

Jeremy waited for them at the register. He shook Hank's hand, then said to Sadie, "So glad you guys could make it. You're just in time to try out my new toy."

Sadie's gaze darted between Hank and Jeremy. "New toy? What new toy?" She faced Hank. "You said nothing about a new toy."

"Not my fault you didn't ask that question."

Her lips turned up in an endearing pout, and both men grinned at her reaction.

"Shall we show her what I've got?" Jeremy asked.

Hank pretended to be deep in thought. "I don't know. Maybe we should drag out the suspense a little longer."

Sadie lightly punched his arm. "You know I hate surprises. Let's go."

Hank relented. "Looks like we'd better show her."

Jeremy laughed and gestured for them to follow him. They skirted around the Christmas tree lot and headed to what looked like an ice skating rink. As they got closer, Sadie released a tiny gasp.

"Oh my gosh, are these bumper cars on ice?"

Jeremy's grin widened. "They are, and they are a lot of fun."

Sadie slapped gloved hands on her hips. "Let me guess, you've already tried them out?"

"Of course. How can I promote it if I haven't tested them myself?"

"Makes sense," Sadie said. "Thumbs up or down?"

Jeremy burst out laughing. "Up of course."

"Well then, what are we waiting for? Get us out there," Sadie said.

Minutes later, they were out on the ice with half a dozen other people sliding and banging into each other.

Sadie's laughter was music to Hank's ears. He especially loved it when she scrunched up her face, floored the accelerator and aimed directly for his car, then sent him spinning off in the opposite direction.

Hank chased after her, sideswiping the back of her car, sending her into a tailspin. Peals of laughter echoed from her.

A family joined them with a group of kids, from preschoolers to preteens. The kids chased after them, and Hank and Sadie played along, laughing uproariously when the kids hit them. They pretended to chase after them, missing the kids intentionally.

Childish laughter filled the air as they chased after the children again, their parents getting into the act, too, until their time was up.

"That's the most fun I've had in ages," Sadie declared, as they exited the cars. "I'm so glad we did this."

Hank nodded his agreement. "Me, too. Are you ready for our next event?"

"Ready and raring to go."

Before they left the bumper cars, they stopped at the snack bar for coffee and pastries before going in search of Jeremy.

"What did you think of it?" Jeremy asked, when they found him in the lot pricing trees.

Sadie's animated expression reminded Hank of his kindergartners when they talked about Santa Claus. "It was so much fun. I loved the whole thing. And the kiddos that were there seemed to be having a great time, too."

Jeremy rocked back on his heels, his hands folded behind his back, obviously pleased with her response. "What about you?" he asked Hank.

"What's not to love? You get to ride in a bumper car, bang into people, and send them spinning all over the place—and it's on ice. Every kid's dream—some adults, too."

Sadie's vigorous nod of agreement was all Jeremy needed.

"What's next?" Sadie asked, rubbing her hands together in anticipation.

Her question brought another laugh from them.

"What would you say to a little cross-country twilight skiing and maybe see the northern lights?" Hank asked.

"I'd love it, but I didn't bring my skis."

Hank grinned. "Well, that's not completely true. I had a little help from Jody and Nick. They gathered together your gear and slipped it into my truck while I was picking you up."

Sadie shook her finger at him. "You are so sneaky." She threw her arms around Hank and whispered into his ear, "I love it."

"What do you say we hit the trail?" Hank asked.

"Let's do it."

CHAPTER 19

One of the things Hank loved most about Sadie was her enthusiasm for everything, whether it was a new project on the farm or taking a late afternoon ski with him. She embraced it all with her whole heart.

They got their gear from the truck, and within minutes, were ready to go.

"I hope you don't mind a little uphill."

"Not at all. Where are we headed?"

Hank pointed to the trail off to their left that steadily climbed upward. "Jeremy says there's a meadow at the top where we might see the northern lights."

"Let's go."

They set off, the late afternoon sun casting a soft glow over them. They steadily climbed the hill, and they were both breathing heavily by the time they crested the top. A herd of elk in the far corner of the meadow looked up, watching them with guarded apprehension.

They skied to the end of the trail. Leaning on her poles, Sadie sighed, taking in the view as the sun dropped over the horizon and darkness settled over the meadow. They didn't have long to wait for the northern lights to appear, turning the sky electric with shades of neon purple, blue, and green.

Sadie leaned into Hank, pressing her lips to his. "This is so beautiful. Thank you for bringing me up here," she said, her voice a soft whisper.

He slid an arm around her waist, pulling her close. "It's amazing, isn't it?" he said, his voice a soft caress against her skin.

Sadie nodded, her body melting into his as the colors reflected over them.

Hank's breath frosted when he turned to speak to her. "What do you say we ski back down and go Christmas caroling before dinner?"

"Isn't it awfully early? I mean it's not even Thanksgiving yet."

"I know, but Marilyn always starts Christmas really early."

A slight hesitation, then she nodded. "Sounds like a perfect pre-dinner activity."

TURNING ON THEIR HEADLAMPS, they took the trail back down, the northern lights glowing over them, making Sadie wish she could spend more time in the country.

When they reached the bottom, they put away their gear and drove to the inn, where a group of carolers were singing *Silent Night* on the porch. They joined in as the group switched to *Jingle Bells,* each one holding a bell.

Diners inside the inn watched, and some even spilled out onto the porch. When they finished, a round of applause echoed over them.

Joy filled Sadie's heart as she stared up at Hank, and something shifted inside her. Something powerful and life-altering that left her giddy and breathless.

She couldn't ever remember feeling like this with Luke.

After they finished the song, Sadie and Hank changed clothes, then Marilyn escorted them to a table in the back near the fireplace. Cinnamon- and clove-scented candles set the holiday mood. A massive Christmas tree blocked their table from the view of other diners, giving them additional privacy in the tiny alcove.

Holiday music played softly in the background as Sadie studied the artfully decorated room. "This is amazing. Did you do all this?" Her arm swept over the room.

Marilyn's smile lit up her face. "I'm so glad you like it, and yes, I did it all."

"Where do you find the time with a brand-new baby?"

"It can be challenging, especially since she's just started crawling, but she follows me around while I work."

The image sent a deep wave of melancholy over Sadie. She shook it off and forced a smile, her gaze sliding over Hank.

Could he be the one to make all her dreams come true?

THEY FINISHED THEIR MEAL, and Jeremy came over with two slices of red velvet cake.

Sadie groaned, laying her hand over her belly. "I'm so full, I don't know if I can eat anything else."

Jeremy waved it under her nose. "How can you resist trying a bite?"

Sadie inhaled, then released a tiny sigh of appreciation before offering a mock frown. "You could've warned me before I ate that entire meal."

Jeremy set the desserts in front of them without a word of apology.

Sadie picked up her fork and took a bite, the flavors bursting in her mouth.

"What do you think?" Marilyn asked, stopping by the table and hooking her arm through Jeremy's.

Hank gave her two thumbs up. "It's delicious. My compliments to the chef."

Sadie nodded her agreement.

"Thank you," Jeremy said.

Sadie's eyes widened. "You made this?"

He nodded. "I can do more than farm Christmas trees."

"You are a man of many talents," Sadie teased.

Jeremy refilled their coffees, then he and Marilyn left them to enjoy their dessert.

Sadie took another bite, savoring the sweet mix. "This is soooo good."

Hank nodded. "It is and worth the bellyache."

Sadie sat back and sipped her coffee, her stomach full to bursting. "This is such a beautiful place. Jeremy and Marilyn have done an incredible job."

"I agree, and they just keep improving it."

Sadie reached over and squeezed his hand. "Thank you for bringing me here. I didn't realize how much I needed to have a day of fun."

"Thank you for coming with me. I had a wonderful time." Hank paused as if he were about to say something more.

"Is something wrong?" Sadie asked.

He shook his head. "No. There's something I want to ask you."

"I don't bite. Fire away."

Still, he hesitated. Finally, he reached for her hand, holding it tight in his, and said, "I'm going to Angel Falls for Thanksgiving, and I'd like you to come and meet my family."

Sadie grew quiet, withdrawing her hand. She didn't do holidays, and most especially family gatherings after her divorce. She'd planned a full holiday celebration with Luke's family only to have it all fall apart in a week before Christmas. She wasn't putting herself through that again.

What could she say without hurting Hank's feelings?

CHAPTER 20

S adie's reaction caught Hank unaware. He'd sensed her hesitation to take their relationship to the next level, but he hadn't expected complete withdrawal.

"Did I say something to upset you?"

Her smile slipped slightly. The casual observer wouldn't have noticed, but Hank had come to know her well enough in the time they'd been dating to recognize the change in her. Rather than press her, he waited for her to respond.

When the silence between them became uncomfortable, she said, "I'm not sure I'm ready to meet your family."

Her honesty stung, but at the same time, he was grateful to hear her true feelings. "Why?"

Her green eyes locked with his as her fingers tightened around the coffee cup. "Meeting your family makes a statement."

Hank didn't deny the truth of that. "It does, but I'm not certain I see the problem. I care about you, so this seems the next logical step unless you don't feel the same way."

Sadie chewed her lower lip. "Honestly, I'm not sure I have what it takes to make a relationship last, if my divorce is any indication." She paused a moment and then continued. "Can you say you're completely over Lydia?"

"I won't deny Lydia hurt me, but I'm ready to move forward. What makes you think you can't make a relationship last?" he countered, not ready to change the subject.

Sadie's gaze didn't falter. "I care about you, too, but I'm scared I'm going to mess this up like I did with my marriage."

Hank reached out and clasped her hand. "I appreciate your frankness, but is it possible your hesitation is more from fear of being hurt?" He stroked her hand. "Is it possible the real reason you don't want to meet my family is you're afraid I'm going to break your heart the same way your husband did?"

Sadie sucked in a startled gasp, but remained silent, which told him his assessment had been spot on. Clearly she chafed at the truths he'd spoken, but he didn't regret the words.

Finally, she said, "I don't know that I can shut down the farm for the holiday weekend. Black Friday brings in some of my best business."

"We could drive up the day before and come home Thanksgiving night," he suggested, but he could see there was more going on than taking care of the farm.

"I don't want you to rush home because of me."

He studied her closely, saw the fear lurking in her eyes. "I understand it would be difficult to leave the farm, but I think it's more than that." He paused, then said, "There's nothing wrong with being scared. Your ex-husband hurt you, and maybe it will take more time for you to move forward." He squeezed her hands. "I'm willing to wait until you're ready. A broken heart takes what it takes to recover. You can't force it. It just is. If that's what's going on, and it's not fear preventing you from moving forward, then it's just that you're not ready. Only you can make that determination, but whatever you decide, I understand, and I will be waiting."

Sadie stared into his eyes for the longest time, then gave a slow nod. "You've given me a lot to consider."

As much as he wanted her to say yes and take a chance on them, she had to want it. He changed the subject to the upcoming holiday parade.

While Hank smiled and laughed, his heart ached because he knew this might be as far as they ever went. And he wanted so much more—he wanted it all because he was falling for her.

THE ENTIRE RIDE HOME, all Sadie could think about was Hank's invitation to spend Thanksgiving with his family. As much as the idea terrified her, she desperately wanted to accept, to be part of a gathering and not be alone on Thanksgiving. To never be alone again.

Isn't that why she'd married Luke? To fill all the loneliness within her.

Yes.

And her neediness was the reason her marriage had failed. No matter how much love Luke gave her, it never filled the black hole within her.

She looked over at Hank, his face visible in the glow of the dash lights. "I'm sorry about turning down your invitation. You're right, I am scared. I-I have feelings for you, and they terrify me."

He merged into the downtown traffic. "Why?"

She paused to consider how much to tell him. Opening up to him, baring her soul, left her open to all the feelings she'd kept bottled up inside, and worse, to more heartbreak.

Was he worth the risk?

Yes.

He pulled up to her house and left the truck running as he waited for her response.

"You terrify me."

His eyebrows arched. "How do I do that?"

"I mean, my feelings for you terrify me," she clarified. "After my parents died, I had no other family. I was completely alone. My foster parents were kind and tried to include me, but it wasn't the same. They weren't my family. When I went to college, I met Luke and fell in love, or so I thought. I think it was more about not being alone than being in love. When he asked me to marry him, I immediately accepted, but deep down I knew it was a mistake. That I wasn't in love with him." She faced Hank. "I don't want to be with you because I don't want to be alone."

The tenderness in his eyes was nearly her undoing. "I'm not asking for forever. I'm asking that you meet my family. Nothing more." He held up a hand as she started to object. "Yes, I know some of my family will read more into it than there is, but we will know the truth—we care about each other and want to see if we have a future together."

When he put it that way, it sounded so logical, and maybe it was. Maybe she was making more out of it than there really was.

"I'm scared," she finally admitted. "I love spending time with you, but I'm afraid I'm not certain I'm accepting your invitation because I want to be with you or I don't want to be alone on Thanksgiving."

Hank's finger brushed over her lower lip. "There's nothing wrong with not wanting to be alone. I don't want you to be alone, but answer me this? Do you enjoy my company?"

"Yes, absolutely."

"Then come with me because you want to spend time with me, and a pleasant side benefit is you won't be alone." He tilted her chin so that their eyes met. "I don't want you to spend the holiday by yourself. Say yes."

Sadie blinked back the tears that had gathered. "Yes," she whispered. "I'll come."

He kissed her, and she didn't care if she had to shut the farm down for the whole weekend. She was taking a chance on them.

CHAPTER 21

As it turned out, Sadie didn't have to shut down the farm. Nick and Jody had heard about Hank's invitation, and they recruited volunteers to help them run the farm while she was gone. And Annie and Jack were keeping Sweet Pea since they were staying in Snowside to celebrate Thanksgiving with Tony instead of going to Angel Falls.

Sadie's heart filled with joy and gratitude. She didn't realize how many friends she had until they volunteered to help out while she was gone.

The week before Thanksgiving, she worked long hours, getting everything in order. While most of the farm was shut down for the winter, Sadie had to stock the store for the holiday weekend, so she either worked in the greenhouse, took care of the animals, or made preserves for the store to fill the shelves.

Tuesday morning, Sadie finished harvesting the lettuce and picked up the basket filled with salad greens, her gaze sweeping over the hydroponic system. She still had the sense it didn't feel like farming, but rather a futuristic flight-to-Mars farming system. Even so, she couldn't deny how well it worked between the water savings and reduced pest pressure, but a part of her missed the cultivation process of traditional farming. She loved working the soil, feeling freshly turned earth filter through her fingers. While she had no intention of converting the entire farm to hydroponic, she couldn't deny that modern science allowed her to farm year-round, which improved her bottom-line and kept the farm in the black.

In fact, everything on the farm had been going exceptionally well—so well that she kept waiting for the other shoe to drop.

Pulling the greenhouse door closed, she quickly zipped her jacket when the wind zapped the warmth from her body.

Trudging through the snow, she took the basket to the kitchen and put it in the cooler, then went to her office, her thoughts turning to Hank. Ever since she'd agreed to spend Thanksgiving in Angel Falls, he'd been by every day after school to help her get the farm ready for her departure. No job had been too demeaning for him, and all he'd taken in return were her kisses.

She fanned her face as the memory of making out with him in the hay slammed her again. She wanted this to be more than casual dating, but she held back. She had to be sure she wasn't using Hank like she had Luke.

Jody greeted her as she stepped inside the deli. The preschooler craft class was currently in session, and Jody had a long table set out with fifteen preschoolers and their mothers each wearing a Thanksgiving headband made from construction paper and turkey feathers they'd obviously created themselves. Childish chatter and the occasional joyful screech filled the room, along with the gurgle of happy mothers.

Jody was a gem, and thanks to her, the classes drew more than enough income for Sadie to hire an event coordinator. There were so many things she needed to do, but mostly she hesitated looking for a replacement because couldn't bear to lose Jody. She'd become family.

Again, her fear of abandonment reared its ugly head.

Sadie slipped off her coat and hung it on the rack.

Jody spotted her and waved her over, a huge smile engulfing her face.

Following her directive, Sadie went over to the group. She laughed and smiled as a toddler made a handprint turkey on the paper, then dipped his hand in the paint again, plastering another on the plastic apron.

Thirty minutes later, Sadie finally took her leave, still laughing at the antics of the group. A busy class, but so much fun.

Would she ever have a family of her own?

Hank?

She brought that thought to an immediate halt. What happened to taking it slow, to making sure her feelings for him went beyond her fear of abandonment? Way too early to go there, especially when they'd been enemies barely a month ago.

She'd done fast and look where that had gotten her.

Dumped and alone just before Christmas.

Still, she couldn't deny that they'd moved far beyond their initial dislike of each other, and to her surprise, they had a lot in common. She'd developed feelings for the man, and it scared her to death.

The thought stopped her cold.

Hank Dabrowski?

That would have been crazy to consider two months ago, but now?

Shaking off the notion, she headed to the back room to slice lunchmeat for the deli.

Hank's help over the last week had not only eased her work-load, but she looked forward to seeing him, catching up on their day, hearing about his students, and what was going on at school, but most of all she couldn't wait for his touch, the way just the rumble of his voice sent desire through her faster than her baby goats could hop a fence.

And those kisses they'd shared. Ooh la, la! The man knew how to set her on fire.

As much as she enjoyed his company, Sadie got the sense that Hank held back parts of himself, too. Maybe he had his own fears to overcome?

He'd had a nasty breakup and shared the bare-bones details with her, but she sensed he'd stopped short of sharing his deeper feelings. What did that say about their relationship if they couldn't share the most painful parts of their lives?

That kind of sharing takes time.

True.

Sadie went to help Dale with the lunch rush and firmly put thoughts of her relationship with Hank aside. They were getting along well, so why spoil it with doubts?

CHAPTER 22

Hank finished stacking the chairs as Nick came back to the classroom after escorting the kids to the bus. "That was a fun day."

Nick always found pleasure in the simplest of things.

"They were a bit rambunctious today, weren't they?"

Nick's eyes twinkled with suppressed mischief. "The understatement of the day." He began gathering containers of crayons, placing them into the cubbyholes. "It's the most excited I've seen them since I've been here."

"It's the holidays. Halloween kicks it off, and it builds from there."

Nick began rolling up the mats they used for rest time. "Now that you mention it, I do remember. As it gets closer to Christmas, it only intensifies."

"Most definitely."

"That makes sense. And can you blame them? Who wouldn't be excited about Santa coming to town?"

Hank leaned a hip against his desk as he considered Nick's comments. He was absolutely right. Why shouldn't they be excited about Christmas and the magic of the holidays?

"You heading over to Sadie's now?"

"I'm going home to pack first, then I'll help her finish up before we leave. I can't tell you how much I appreciate you and Jody taking over so she can join my family for Thanksgiving."

Nick shrugged off his gratitude. "We're happy to do it, and we're looking forward to this weekend."

"Then I'll see you there."

Nick waved goodbye and disappeared out the door.

Hank grabbed his briefcase and locked the door, then went to his truck, his thoughts turning to this weekend. His mother had called numerous times since he'd told her Sadie was coming to Angel Falls. She was excited to meet her, and Hank couldn't wait to introduce Sadie to his mother and siblings, but most of all, he wanted an entire weekend with her. He enjoyed spending time with her—he just liked being with her. And that scared the hell out of him because he'd liked spending time with Lydia and look how that ended.

Not the same.

He'd developed deep feelings for Sadie, and he couldn't figure out what came next.

Maybe there was nothing to do about it. Maybe it just was what it was.

Hank started his truck, then paused to consider the voice. It was too late to do anything about it because he'd already fallen head over heels for her.

NICK ARRIVED as Jody wrapped up her craft session. Once they were alone, she turned to him. "How's it going with Hank?"

He smoothed his mustache. "Exceptionally well."

"Is he still holding back?" Jody asked.

"No, and I think this weekend will bring them even closer."

Jody thrummed her fingers on the tabletop as her eyes took on a conniving twinkle. "I believe you're right, and maybe we can give them a little nudge in the right direction."

"What have you got in mind?"

"I'm thinking maybe they need some alone time together—just the two of them."

"That's a grand idea. I'll make sure there's space available for them at *The Inn*." Nick made a call, and minutes later he hung up. "All set."

"Excellent. Now all we have to do is stall them a little longer, so they'll have to stop for the night."

"What have you got in mind?"

HANK ARRIVED at the farm a little after four and went straight to the kitchen in search of Sadie.

Empty, and Sadie was nowhere in sight.

Odd, she'd texted that she'd started the food prep for the deli, and by now, she should have been well underway.

He turned and headed to her office.

Empty.

Hank retraced his footsteps and went outside. Shoving his hands into his pockets, he put his head down as fat snowflakes pelted his face. He sighed. It would be a slow drive to Angel Falls tonight.

Reaching the greenhouse, he pulled open the door, the wind nearly ripping it out of his hands. He found Sadie inside, talking with a man.

Sadie looked up, caught his eye, and smiled a warm welcome. Suddenly, he was drowning in her and completely forgot about anything else but her.

"Hank." She waved at him, urging him forward.

He made his way down the rows of lettuce and acknowledged he'd been attracted to her from the moment he met her.

He reached for her, and she raised up on tiptoe to kiss him. A sweet kiss that lingered on his lips long after she stepped back and slid her hand into his. She lowered her voice. "I'm so glad you're here."

Emotions overwhelmed him, and it took a moment for him to pull himself together. Holding out his hand to the other man, he said, "Hank Dabrowski."

"Peter Sims."

"Peter's troubleshooting my system. We had a hiccup today—a leak in the system, and a blockage in the pump."

Hank gazed down at her. "Did you lose any of the crop?"

Sadie shook her head. "Everything's fine, and Peter's been working to get me back on track so it doesn't happen again. Unfortunately, I still have to do the prep work for the deli." She glanced out the window to the snow gathering on the pane. "If you can't wait, I'll understand."

Disappointment zipped across her face. Clearly, she still wanted to go with him.

"Tell me what needs to be done, and I'll take care of it while you finish up here." No way was he going without her.

Sadie's gaze shot up to his, gratitude shimmering in the green depths, leaving him unaccountably joyful. "Are you sure? I should be done in another hour."

"Positive. You do what you need to do. I'll work on slicing the meat, and I'll see if Jody and Nick can help, too."

Sadie flung her arms around his neck and squeezed, her breath warming his ear. "Thank you. I don't know how I'd get it all done without you."

"Anything for you, Sadie—anything."

She pulled back and the sudden loss of warmth chilled him

more than the icy wind blowing outside. But the gratitude shimmering in her eyes told him everything he needed to know.

Hank headed back to the main building, feeling like the luckiest guy on the planet because Sadie was his girl.

SADIE WATCHED Hank disappear out the door, her shoulders relaxing for the first time all day. She had help. Hank was here to ease her burden, and he was willing to wait for her. With him, Nick, and Jody, she knew the deli would be ready in no time. But more than that, appreciation swept through her.

"What do we need to do to get this up and running, Peter?" she asked.

Sadie had plans, and nothing would keep her from meeting Hank's family.

CHAPTER 23

Thanksgiving Weekend

Full darkness had settled over the farm when Hank and Sadie finally headed out of the city. With the windshield wipers on high, Hank peered through the windshield, trying to stay on the road as the snow came down sideways.

"Do you think we ought to turn around?" Sadie asked.

"I would if I could find an exit, but it's at least ten miles to the next one. I was thinking we should find a hotel for the night. Can you search online and see if there's anything close?"

Hank waited while she studied her phone. "Anything?"

"The only thing I can find is a bed-and-breakfast at the next exit. I'm going to call and see if they have any rooms."

She put it on speaker, and after three rings, a female voice answered.

"Pine Cove Inn."

"Hello, I was calling to find out if you had any rooms available tonight?"

"Let me check." A moment later, she came back on the line.

"We had a cancellation for our two-room suite. It's the only room we have left."

Sadie glanced at Hank and he nodded.

"We'll take it," she said.

They arrived at the inn twenty minutes later to learn that the room and dinner were paid for in full.

The couple who'd reserved it had to cancel, and instead of taking a refund, they asked the owners to pay it forward.

She and Hank protested and insisted on paying, but the owner refused to accept their money. Finally, they took the keys to the suite. Hank carried both bags up three flights of stairs, and he did so without breaking a sweat. Sadie would have been huffing and puffing by the second floor, with only her bag.

They reached the third floor, and Sadie unlocked the door. Her breath caught as she stepped into the suite. A small sofa and box chair were next to the fireplace, which cast a warm glow over the room. To the left, a counter with a mini fridge underneath and a cupboard above, then two doors leading to the bedrooms, each with their own private bath.

She turned to him. "It's beautiful, don't you think?"

Hank set the bags down as his gaze swept the room. "It's nice."

Sadie rolled her eyes. Men, she thought. Then she looked deeply into his eyes, and the heat of his gaze told her he was more interested in her than the room. Now, how could she be annoyed about that?

Suddenly nervous, she licked her lips. "Let me freshen up, and we can go down to dinner."

Taking the bedroom on her left, she grabbed her suitcase and escaped the sudden rush of feelings. Tossing her suitcase on the bed, she unzipped it, and took her overnight case into the bathroom, then froze. The bathroom looked as if it had come straight off the pages of *Martha Stewart Living* magazine, from the claw foot tub to the massive tiled shower.

What would it be like to soak in that tub with Hank? Oh no, she was not going there. Her pace might be incredibly slow for the twenty-first century, but she wouldn't allow her hormones to take the lead this time.

She opened her bag, quickly touched up her makeup, and added a quick swipe of blush to her cheeks, even though thoughts of sharing the suite with Hank had already heightened her color.

She stared at her reflection. What she really wanted was to share that king size bed with him.

No, no, no. That was a major step, and one she wasn't ready to take—yet—but she sure wanted to.

Instead, she changed into a dark burgundy sweater that, according to Annie, highlighted her best assets.

She walked into the sitting room to find Hank relaxing in the chair next to the window. His eyes lit up when he saw her, and his reaction told her Annie had been spot on about the sweater.

He crossed over to her. "You look amazing," he said. Fire flashed in his eyes as his gaze swept over her again before he dipped his head and captured her lips, sucking the breath from her. He trailed kisses along her jaw all the way to the tender spot behind her ear, leaving her breathless and achy with need.

When he lifted his head, his eyes were dark with a yearning that matched her own. Her lips tilted into a lopsided smile. "I'll have to remember to wear this sweater more often."

Hank's gaze swept over her as if just noticing it for the first time, then shifted back to her eyes as his hands tightened around her waist. "You look beautiful whether you're wearing jeans and a T-shirt from work or dressed for a fancy dinner."

The sincerity of his expression seared into her. Her fingertips brushed over his shoulders. "So, handsome, what do you say we go eat?"

He grinned, and it deepened the blue of his eyes, sending heat rushing through Sadie again. "A woman after my heart."

How was she going to keep it platonic tonight when just a kiss lit her off like a fireworks display on the Fourth of July?

Hank escorted her downstairs, the scent of gingerbread and pine drifting up the stairwell. A Christmas tree decorated with strings of popcorn and cranberries, and velvet red bows sat in front of the bay window. The hostess led them to an intimately set table tucked away in the far corner beside the fireplace. A cluster of dancing elves sat on the mantel with garland looped over the edges.

The hostess handed them menus and departed with their drink order.

"This place is amazing. I don't know how we lucked into getting a room tonight. Can you believe it's paid in full, including the meal?" Sadie asked.

"I can't."

"It was certainly nice of whoever couldn't make it to gift the room and meal to us," she said.

"It was," Hank agreed.

The waitress arrived with their wine, pouring them each a glass and promising to return to take their order.

Hank lifted his glass. "To a memorable weekend."

Their glasses clinked, and Sadie's thoughts raced to the night ahead. "This is a big step we're taking. Are you ready for it?"

"We discussed this. I want you to meet my family, but I'm not pressuring you to take our relationship to the next level."

She hadn't been referring to his family. She'd been thinking about spending the night alone with him in their suite. "I'm looking forward to meeting them."

His eyes never left hers. "They want to meet you, too," he said.

Sadie hoped that was the case, but what if she didn't compare to his ex-fiancée? Would Hank's mother welcome her or resent her for taking Lydia's place?

He reached across the table and squeezed her hand as if reading her thoughts. "My mother is going to love you."

Sadie's heart lightened at his reassurance. She hadn't realized she needed to hear those words until he'd said them. Everything would work out so long as she had Hank by her side.

CHAPTER 24

They finished eating and lingered over cocktails. Couples glided onto the dance floor. When a slow melody played, Hank rose and took Sadie into his arms. Swaying to the music, he felt as nervous as the first time he kissed Mary Jo Porter at their eighth-grade dance. Then, he'd been drenched in perspiration. He wasn't quite that anxious with Sadie, but his pulse still beat like a jackhammer.

He wanted Sadie more than he'd wanted any woman he'd dated, even Lydia. While Hank had loved Lydia, deep down he'd known they weren't right for each other even before she tried to swindle his mother. Self-centered, his ex only thought of herself. If only he'd recognized that sooner, it might've saved him a lot of heartache.

The past was the past. His future was with Sadie—or so he hoped. And tonight, well, he didn't know what it would bring, but he desperately wanted her to be alone with her.

They finished another dance, and he couldn't wait a moment longer to have her all to himself. They entered the suite minutes later, the lamp casting a soft, romantic glow over the sitting room. He closed the door, and Sadie faced him. She sucked in a breath when he swept her into his arms and did what he'd wanted to do all through dinner—kiss her.

He swallowed her moan. His hands lifted her sweater where all that warm, silky skin waited for his touch.

"Hank."

Her voice barely penetrated his lust-starved brain. Finally, he found the wherewithal to pull back, his hands sliding to her wrists.

She stared at him, her eyes dark with desire, but something else undefinable. "I care about you, Hank. I want you so much, but I'm not ready to take this step. I have to be sure I don't repeat past mistakes."

He tucked a stray lock of hair behind her ear. "Won't happen."

"You can't possibly know that."

"I'm certain of it because I'm not Luke."

She shook her head. "You don't understand."

"Then explain it to me."

She swallowed, the pulse at the base of her throat throbbing. "I rushed into a relationship with my ex-husband, and it ended in disaster. I won't survive another breakup like that." Her gaze pleaded for understanding.

"What happened?"

Her eyes glistened with unshed tears. "Could I tell you when we get back? I don't want to ruin our trip with painful memories."

He really wanted to know now, but he'd give her the time she asked for. He kissed her once more, a sweet kiss that hinted at the barely restrained passion burning within him. She was the one he'd been searching for. Whatever happened going forward, they would figure it out—together.

SADIE WATCHED Hank go into his room and wanted desperately to join him, but memories of Luke and their breakup stopped her. There was no way she'd escape the memories tonight, but she'd held Hank off a bit longer with her impassioned plea. How long that would work, she didn't know, but she'd stall as long as she could.

She went to her room and changed into her pajamas as the past rushed at her from all sides. She'd met Luke her third year in college, and she'd immediately fallen for him. They'd had so much in common. Both entomology students, they could talk about insects for hours, and they'd both loved hiking and biking. A perfect match, or so Sadie thought at the time.

They went from friends to lovers shortly after meeting and moved in together a month later. And two months after that, Luke proposed. A whirlwind romance that felt perfect until it started to unravel after graduation. They'd both gotten jobs at the university and Sadie's career took off, while Luke's stalled. It became a bone of contention between them. He became more distant as the holidays approached. A week before Christmas she stopped by his lab with a picnic dinner since they'd both been working long hours and had seen little of each other. But instead of a romantic dinner with her husband, she found him making out with a grad student.

Crushed, she'd left. He caught up with her and told her it was all her fault. She'd pushed him into marriage when he wasn't ready to settle down, and he needed his freedom.

While she knew she wasn't solely to blame, his words had struck a nerve. She couldn't deny that when they'd met, she'd been desperately lonely, and he'd filled that emptiness within her.

She left him and never looked back, but his words still scarred her all these years later. While she cared about Hank, she couldn't risk their budding relationship by rushing it.

She crawled into bed certain she wouldn't sleep, but the next thing she knew dawn filtered through the curtains.

Sadie rolled onto her back and stretched. Looking out the window, heavy, dense clouds filled the sky.

She heard the shower running and visions of Hank, naked under the spray of water, tormented her. Pushing the image aside, she pulled on her clothes and brushed her teeth.

She'd just finished getting ready when the water shut off. Rolling her suitcase into the sitting room, she started a pot of coffee.

Hank's voice whispered over her, sending chills racing over her skin. "Good morning, beautiful."

She slowly turned to him. "Good morning, handsome," she murmured. "I'm making coffee for the road. I was thinking they might have something in the bakery downstairs we could take to eat on the way."

Hank's gaze flickered over her. The absolute last thing she wanted was to leave their private haven. What she really wanted was to forget the past and haul him into the bedroom, but she didn't.

"Much as I'd like to stay here with you, you're right, we really should get moving."

Sadie's heart warmed as the disappointment in his voice echoed her own.

"Coffee and something from the bakery sounds perfect," he said.

"It should be done brewing any minute."

He leaned down and twined a lock of her hair around his finger, drawing her against him. "First, I need a good morning kiss."

Sadie happily complied, and his kiss turned her into an inferno of need. Pulling back, her voice shook. "That probably wasn't the best idea."

"Probably not, but I'd do it again."

Sadie would, too, but she didn't dare because it would only

complicate the situation. She needed to be sure of his feelings for her before they took the next step in their relationship.

Hank cleared his throat. "Why don't you get our coffees together, and I'll take our bags to the truck?"

Sadie nodded, taking a moment to pull herself together. "Sugar, no cream, right?"

Rather than kiss her again, he rubbed his nose to hers. "Right," he said, then disappeared out the door. His exit made the room feel small and lonely.

THEY ARRIVED in Angel Falls a little after nine. Hank's mother swept Sadie into a warm, welcoming hug.

"Thank you so much for inviting me, Mrs. Dabrowski," Sadie said, as Hank's mom led her back to the airy country kitchen.

Once his mom heard they'd only had coffee since the bakery was closed, she insisted on feeding them.

"Call me Sally, and I'm just so pleased you could join us. I was afraid you wouldn't be able to get away from the farm."

"I almost didn't," Sadie admitted. "There was a problem with the greenhouse, and if not for Hank stepping in to help, I'd probably still be there."

"Well, I'm so glad it all worked out."

"Me, too." Sadie glanced over at Hank with adoring eyes.

"Hank, pour the girl some coffee and get her settled at the bar, while I get you two some breakfast."

"Do you have time for that, Mom? I can make us breakfast."

She hugged him, her trim body engulfed by his larger one. Sadie guessed she was well into her fifties, but she sure couldn't tell by looking at her. Her dark locks, the same color as her son's, glistened in the low light, not a strand of gray to be seen. She wore just enough makeup to enhance her features, but not over-power her face.

She shooed Hank away. "It's already made. I've been keeping it warm for stragglers."

"Is that what you think of us?" Hank teased.

His mother shook a spatula at him, her eyes on Sadie. "Don't you listen to a word he says. You are not a straggler." Her eyes danced with merriment when she focused on her son. "Him, I'm not so sure about."

Good-natured teasing filled the kitchen, and Sadie recalled the same banter with her parents.

The Grinch reared its head again.

See, I told you the holidays only bring back memories best forgotten.

Sadie pushed the Grinch back into Whoville, determined to have a memorable weekend with Hank and his family.

THE REST of Hank's relatives, except for Elroy who was spending the holiday in Snowside serving Thanksgiving dinner for the homeless, and Annie, drifted in one by one until the room was full to bursting with children racing around, giggling and shouting with glee. Sadie immediately fell in love with his entire family.

She couldn't imagine living so far away from them if she were Hank. If she had a family like this, she'd move closer. The rest of the Murphy Clan, as they called themselves, descended late morning with first and second cousins, aunts and uncles, nieces and nephews. Some had even flown in from Paradise Falls, Idaho. Hank's cousin-in-law, Seth McKenzie, owned a Christmas tree farm, and Sadie discovered they had a lot in common.

"So, you're the urban farmer," Seth said, after they'd been introduced.

"And you raise Christmas trees."

"I do."

"I have a friend who has a Christmas tree farm about a half hour out of Snowside. He and his wife also run a restaurant and inn that's doing really well."

"That's interesting because we're expanding our operation with the hopes it will become a destination spot. We have Christmas trees we sell starting the day after Thanksgiving. Santa Claus, sleigh rides, and hot chocolate are available. We strive to make it a family event, but we're also starting a winter festival this year, sleigh rides on Valentine's Day, that kind of thing. We're still working out our summer events."

"How did you manage to be here with opening day tomorrow?" Sadie would love to have more time away without having to shut down the farm or depend on friends to operate it while she was gone.

"My dad's filling in for me. We're partners."

That explained it.

"Do you run the whole farm on your own?" Seth asked.

"I have some seasonal help, but mostly, it's just me."

Seth shook his head. "Take my advice, as soon as finances permit, hire permanent help. You won't regret it."

Sadie didn't doubt it, but it was hard to hire more employees other than an event planner when she had cash flow issues. Rather than admit that, she changed the subject. "I got a grant last year to convert my greenhouse into a hydroponic system."

"What do you think of it?" Seth asked with genuine interest.

"I like it, but it's not the kind of farming I love."

He studied her for a long moment. "Ah, you're one of those who loves the feel of the dirt sifting through your fingers, aren't you?"

Sadie flushed. "Guilty," she admitted, a bit sheepishly.

"Nothing wrong with that, but I'm guessing there are advantages to hydroponic farming."

"There are, which is why I gave in and converted the greenhouse. Now I have produce year-round."

"A fair tradeoff, wouldn't you say?"

"Absolutely. Do you raise any crops besides Christmas trees?" Sadie asked.

"Not really. We have some horses, but farming is more my dad's thing. I make furniture and Frankie, my wife, builds toys." He gestured to the woman in animated conversation with Hank's mother.

"How interesting. Do you have a website?"

"We do." Seth handed her a card with their website address on it.

"I'll check this out. Thanks."

"How did you get into farming?" Seth asked.

Sadie launched into how she'd met Elroy and gone from renting to farming the land and her struggles with financing.

"We were having similar problems, and it can be a real pain dealing with bureaucracy, so Dad contacted our local representative. I think you made a smart move reaching out to yours. You fit all the criteria for a federal loan, but government agencies can't see around their rules to make it work. A member of congress, on the other hand, can put pressure on them."

"I sure hope you're right." Sadie said.

"When you're a small operation, you need someone with political clout."

"Seth," Frankie called out.

"The boss is calling." He left her with a wink and a wave.

Sadie started for the kitchen, but when she turned, she bumped into a very large, very warm body—Hank. His arm snaked around her waist. "I've been looking for you."

The deep tenor of his voice vibrated inside her. "I've been right here talking to Seth."

"Let me guess, you two were discussing farming."

"We were."

"Then you need to speak to my other cousin, Max, who runs the maple tree farm here in town—The Sticky Bucket."

Sadie arched a brow. "The Sticky Bucket. I like it."Hank gestured to a tall, dark-haired man, laughing with his mom.

"Introduce me."

Hank's eyes lit with the devil. "Later. Right now, I want some alone time with you."

Sadie fanned her face as heat raced over her cheeks when she considered what that alone time might entail.

"Oh my," she whispered.

CHAPTER 25

The meal was delicious, the company fabulous. Sadie saw exactly where Hank got his vibrant personality from after hearing all the stories about his dad as they feasted on the traditional meal of turkey, stuffing, mashed potatoes and gravy, homemade rolls that melted in your mouth, and a dozen other dishes she didn't have room to sample.

After the dishes were cleared away, the games began. She and Hank paired up against Frankie and Seth, and Hank's brother, Walt, and sister-in-law, Toni.

Sadie and Hank won four of the five games they played. They seemed to have a knack for reading each other, and Sadie found herself falling a little harder for him. A man who loved his family was a gem, but a man who could read her was an absolute treasure.

Why did she resist giving him her heart?

SADIE WOKE up the next morning and glanced at the bedside clock.

Eight-fifteen.

She rarely slept past six, but today of all days, she'd slept in, and they were going to cut Christmas trees! From what she'd been told the night before, it was tradition in Hank's family to drive into the forest and cut Christmas trees together.

Throwing back the covers, she scrambled out of bed. She wouldn't hold up the outing. After a quick shower, she dressed, and applied minimal makeup, then went downstairs to discover only a few people milling around.

Had they gone without her?

She walked into the kitchen and discovered Hank making breakfast. "You're up early. I thought you'd sleep in," he said.

Sadie laughed. "This is sleeping in for me. Where is everyone?"

"Sleeping."

Relieved and shocked, she asked, "So I didn't miss cutting Christmas trees?"

Hank set down the spatula and tucked her into his arms, running his fingers through her hair. "Did you really think I'd go off and leave you?"

Sadie shrugged, suddenly embarrassed. "Well, your mom did say she wanted to get up there early."

Hank's laughter rang out, the sound resonating deep within her. "Early for Mom would be making it there by noon."

"Oh, I didn't realize that."

"I should've made that clear last night, then you could have slept later."

Sadie shook her head. "Unlikely."

"Something I'm going to have to work on then," Hank murmured with a suggestive wink before turning back to check the sausage.

Sadie huffed out a breath. "Not likely. My parents told me even as a kid I was up with the sun."

Hank cracked eggs into a bowl. "Tell me about your parents."

She seldom talked about them, and it struck her how wrong it felt not to. She'd loved them with a desperation that left her empty inside, and they'd loved her.

"My dad was a chemistry teacher at Snowside High. He loved the outdoors and taught me everything about insects and reptiles. My mom told me I'd toddle after him, begging to hunt for skinks and butterflies. As I got older, I'd spend time at Mom's flower shop. She taught me all about growing plants." A sense of peace settled over her as she told him about her parents, recalling the good times they'd had.

"It sounds like you were close."

"We were. I wish you could have met them."

"Me, too."

She leaned into him, watching as he expertly whisked the pancake batter. "I like your family."

He rubbed the tip of his nose against hers, making her smile.

"What can I do to help?" she asked.

Hank nodded to the fruit stacked up on the counter. "Those need to be sliced."

Sadie took the apron off the hook and began peeling a mango. She couldn't help but notice they worked well together—another plus in the Hank Department. The man had an awful lot of pluses beside his name.

Sounds like a keeper, as Annie would say.

Seth and Frankie came into the kitchen a few minutes later and began helping with the meal. Unbeknownst to Sadie, Hank had breakfast duty. Apparently, his mother assigned meals to each person. Sadie thought that was a brilliant way to handle feeding so many people. She would have to take notes from his mom. Those were the organizational skills she needed in an event coordinator.

"How far is it to where you cut Christmas trees?" Sadie asked.

"Not far," Frankie said, heating the syrup. "Maybe ten minutes, wouldn't you say?" she asked Hank.

"Yes, something like that. It's not like Snowside, where we have to drive thirty minutes or more depending on traffic just to get out of the city."

"Well, this Christmas tree farmer thinks we should support the farms by going to the lot to get a tree," Seth announced.

Frankie rolled her eyes. "I think Christmas tree farms are surviving just fine, and don't forget, very few people are going out and cutting their own trees anymore."

"Says you," Seth shot back.

Hank nodded his agreement.

Sadie raised up on tiptoe and pressed a kiss to Hank's cheek, her eyes gleaming with laughter. "If you want, we can stop at Jeremy's on the way home, but I want to go on the outing with everyone else and cut a tree. I'm not missing this."

For once, her inner Grinch remained silent.

Hank's fiery gaze sent a flash of heat straight to her core. "Your wish is my command."

SINCE SADIE, Hank, Seth, and Frankie cooked breakfast, the cleanup crew took care of the breakfast dishes and another group prepared the food to take for their outing. Sadie was more and more impressed with Hank's mother. She had an entire system in place for cooking and cleanup, and Sadie made plenty of mental notes.

Sally entered the kitchen after Hank went upstairs to shower and change. She poured a cup of coffee and topped off Sadie's. "Since everyone is busy, let's sit and talk while they get ready."

She led her to a pair of chairs off the kitchen in what Sadie had heard referred to as the sunroom. It had a view of Angel

Falls, and she could see rooftops covered in snow with smoke trailing from the chimneys, creating a picture-perfect setting. "It's so beautiful," Sadie said.

Sally sipped her coffee and stared out at rows of quaint houses. "It is beautiful, but sometimes I get the urge to leave here. Do something new."

Sadie studied the older woman. "Really? All your family is here."

"They are, and that keeps me from leaving. Don't get me wrong, I love Angel Falls. Love my family, but I'd like to spread my wings a little."

"And do what?" Sadie asked.

"I'm not sure. I'm retiring in January."

Hank had mentioned she'd worked as the school secretary from the time his youngest sister started school nearly three decades ago. Sadie could certainly understand the need for a change.

"Are you going to do some traveling?"

"I've considered it, but I'm not fond of traveling alone."

Sadie understood that, too.

"Enough about me. I want to hear about this farm of yours. I looked it up online before I went to sleep last night, and it's just lovely."

Sadie blushed with pleasure. "Thank you. It's my little slice of paradise."

"It looks that way. A vast difference from Elroy's weed-infested piece of ground. Why didn't you bring Sweet Pea?"

She must have seen the photo of her and Sweet Pea on the welcome page. "Annie offered to keep her, and Zoe adores her."

"Ah, that makes sense. I was hoping to meet her after all the stories Elroy's told me about Sweet Pea."

"She loves Elroy, and so do I. He's helped make my dreams

come true." Sadie rocked and sipped her coffee, enjoying the peaceful moment.

"Mom." A moment later, Addie, Hank's youngest sister, popped her head around the corner. She saw Sadie and immediately apologized for interrupting them.

"No worries," Sadie assured her. "I need to get ready."

She bid the women goodbye and went up to her room, envying Hank and all his family.

CHAPTER 26

An hour later, Sadie climbed into Hank's truck with Frankie and Seth in the back seat. They caravanned with the rest of Hank's family to the mountain in search of perfect trees. Driving up a windy road, they came to a snow-covered meadow and parked.

Young and old, everyone wore snowshoes, except the tiny ones strapped into backpacks. Sadie marveled at the generations of the Murphy Clan, all laughing and teasing each other as they set off.

Hank's mom chose the first tree she'd seen after searching every square inch of the meadow, much to everyone's amusement.

Hank's warm breath whispered in Sadie's ear, "Same thing happens every year."

The twinkle in his eye told her he didn't mind, and that it was part and parcel of who his mom was.

A man who loved his mother dearly. Was there anything more appealing?

"You know, I find it incredibly sexy the way you admire your mother."

Hank arched an inquisitive eyebrow at her. "Why?"

Sadie drew back to look into his eyes. "Why wouldn't I? Some men don't."

Hank studied her for a long moment. "Like Luke?"

The years rolled away to the days when Luke's family enveloped her into their fold. The love they'd shown her. "No. Luke loved his family, and it was part of my attraction to him. I was actually thinking of the men I've dated over the years who weren't close to their families."

"Is that why it didn't work out with them?"

Sadie pondered his question. "It might have been part of it, but we just didn't connect."

A partial truth. The whole truth was, she wanted a man who loved her and none of them had.

SADIE FOUND a quiet corner and watched as they set up the tree and started decorating that evening. *Not Christmas*, her Grinch cried out. It was one thing to go on an outing, another to decorate a tree and bring up memories best left forgotten.

Sally came and sat beside her while the children strung popcorn and cranberries for the tree.

Smiling, Sally said, "You're welcome to join in."

Sadie shook her head. "Thanks. I'm enjoying watching everyone else."

Electric blue eyes studied her. "Christmas isn't always an easy time," she murmured softly.

A sudden rush of tears clogged Sadie's throat.

Sally squeezed her hand and rocked. "Leroy, Hank's dad died mid-summer, and even though I knew it was coming, I was so lost. I wanted to curl into a ball and just shut out the world, but I couldn't. I had five children that needed me to be strong. So, I picked myself up and kept going. I did okay until fall. I dreaded the coming holiday and even the kids were subdued. None of us wanted to face it without Leroy."

"What did you do?"

Sally's smile turned brittle. "I fell apart. You can only deny your feelings for so long. Fortunately, all the family gathered round and helped us through."

"Does it ever get better?"

Sally's eyes darkened with sympathy. "The next holiday was easier, and the next, but it never quite feels normal."

"It's like there's a hole inside."

"Yes, that's it exactly." She paused, then asked, "Did you lose someone?"

"Yes. My parents died in a car accident when I was sixteen." She didn't mention her breakup with Luke. For some reason, that was even more painful.

Sally nodded, staring into the fire. "Some losses are harder than others. Losing a child or a parent isn't easy. Did you have family to help you?"

Sadie shook her head. "It was just me."

Hank's mother remained silent for long minutes as she watched the children throwing as much popcorn as they strung. "That's hard."

Sadie nodded. "My foster parents were kind and tried to include me in their family, but it just wasn't the same. After college, I started renting from Elroy, and he took me in and included me in his holiday activities, but I'm sure Elroy has already told you that."

"I knew you'd moved in and started a farm, but not the rest."

The squeak of the rocker filled the intervening silence. Sadie found the rhythm comforting.

"Gibby, come help us," a childish voice shouted at Sally, the name her grandchildren called her.

"Be right there." She turned to Sadie. "Will you be okay?"

"I'm fine. Go on and enjoy."

The caring and concern in her expression filled Sadie with pleasure. Oh, what she wouldn't give to have a family like this of her very own.

HANK REMAINED IN THE SHADOWS. He'd intended to join Sadie and his mom, but hesitated when they discussed her parents. Eavesdropping was wrong, but after hearing their conversation, he was determined to give Sadie a Christmas she'd never forget.

EARLY SUNDAY MORNING, Hank and Sadie said their goodbyes to his family, then stopped at the Angel Falls Mini Mart to gas the truck. Sadie went inside to get coffee for the road, and she came out to find him talking with a woman—a very attractive woman—the kind of woman Luke would have been drawn to. More than pretty, she was drop-dead gorgeous. Dark hair and eyes with a body curved in all the right places, and that face with the pert nose, high cheekbones, and perfectly placed dimples would attract any man.

Not Hank. He wouldn't cheat on her.

She'd thought the same thing about Luke.

"You drove me to this. I wouldn't have turned to other women if you hadn't been so needy." Luke's final jab still stung ten years later.

She pushed aside the memory. Pasting on a smile, she squared her shoulders, and walked over to him, clutching the paper tray holding their coffee in one hand and the bag of pastries in the other.

As she approached, she noted Hank's pinched expression, his

lips pressed tight with anger. He gave Sadie a curt nod, and in the stilted silence that fell between the three of them, she fidgeted.

Finally, the woman said, "I should be going. It was good seeing you again, Hank." She sized Sadie up before climbing into her Mercedes and driving off.

Hank didn't introduce them, and Sadie suspected she knew the reason. That had been his ex—Lydia.

His gaze narrowed as he watched her drive away, then he blinked as if the encounter had been nothing more than seeing an old acquaintance. Removing the hose from the gas tank, he waited for the receipt to print, then climbed into the truck.

Sadie hesitated a moment, then got in, snapped her seatbelt, and moments later, they set off. Rather than play coy, she said, "So, that was Lydia."

Hank cast a sidelong glance her direction before turning his attention back to the road. "That was her."

His voice lacked emotion, which Sadie suspected hid the emotions churning within him.

"She's very attractive."

Hank grunted, but didn't respond. Maybe he was hoping she'd drop the subject.

Foolish man. Hank should have known she didn't back down from uncomfortable subjects unless, of course, it was about her. "So, what did she have to say?"

Hank blew out of beleaguered breath and smiled, but it was more of a grimace. "You're not gonna let this go, are you?"

Sadie shot him a sassy grin. "Not a chance. Would you, if the situation were reversed?"

CHAPTER 27

Hank debated how to explain his feelings for Lydia. Anger and resentment flared hot and heavy in his gut, mostly because she'd managed to trample his masculinity in five minutes flat.

How did she do that? And how did he tell Sadie that he'd loved a woman who'd done nothing but hurt him and could still strip him raw with just a few words? What would she think of him?

"Lydia reminded me of how lucky I am that I broke it off with her."

Sadie faced him, her brows arching in question.

"I surprised you with that comment, didn't I?"

"You did. Does that mean you're not interested in getting back together with her?"

The words settled inside of him like a stone sinking to the bottom of a lake. "Absolutely not."

Sadie said nothing, and her silence told him she wanted more, that his answer hadn't satisfied her. Rather than explain, he changed the subject. "What's in the bag?"

Disappointment or hurt, he couldn't be sure what emotion

flared in her eyes, then vanished when she smiled. Opening the bag, she held it toward him.

The scent of maple filled the interior of the truck.

"They had maple bars made from maple syrup straight from The Sticky Bucket, except I got the maple bites."

She held one to his lips, and he bit into it, his tongue sweeping over her fingers.

She froze, and her eyes widened.

That had been no accident. He'd wanted to taste her.

Looking away, she took another from the bag and popped it into her mouth. Her eyes lit with obvious pleasure. "Oh my God, that's to die for."

Hank nodded his agreement, and she offered him another, but instead of feeding it to him, she held it out to him.

Their eyes locked again before he took it from her.

When they finished the bag, Sadie rubbed her stomach. "Those were the perfect ending to a wonderful trip. Thank you for bringing me. I love your family. You have what I've wanted for as long as I can remember."

Hank cast a sidelong glance at her. "They loved you, too." He threaded his fingers through hers.

Her eyes glistening with unshed tears, she said, "Thank you. I loved every minute."

Hank squeezed her hand, wanting to spend every holiday with her.

HANK HEADED to the farm right after school on Thursday to see Sadie. He found her and Jody in the kitchen as they finished making a batch of jam. He sniffed the air, and his stomach gave an appreciative rumble. "That smells delicious."

"Even better on one of those scones that came from the scone shop around the corner," Jody said.

"Sold."

Jody smiled. "It's time we took a break, anyway. I'll rustle up some scones and coffee. You two bring the jam and meet me in the main room." She disappeared out the door, the dogs leaping up and following her.

Sadie grabbed a jar of blackberry jam, and they went to the dining area where they found two scones and two cups of coffee on the table next to the fireplace, and Sweet Pea sound asleep on her bed. "I sense Jody's playing Cupid—again. What do you think?" Sadie asked.

"Jody always has something up her sleeve," Hank agreed.

"She does. Did she tell you about her plans for Christmas on Ice?"

Hank split open a scone and slathered it with butter and blackberry preserves. "She did."

Sadie poured cream into her coffee. "What do you think?"

"I love it, but do you have time to take on a project of that magnitude?"

"Apparently I'm not taking it on. Jody has it all under control. My only job is to run a booth at the event."

"That sounds doable."

Sadie sipped her coffee, her gaze unfocused. "I don't know what I'm going to do when she leaves."

"No luck finding a replacement?" Hank asked.

"I haven't advertised."

"Why not?"

She hitched a shoulder. "I don't have a lot of time."

"True, but that's not the reason, is it?"

"No." Sadie broke off a piece of scone, but didn't eat it.

"What's the real reason?"

"I don't want Jody to leave."

Hank stroked his fingers over the back of her hand. "I understand. I don't want to lose Nick, either." Silence, then, "What would you say to you, me, and Sweet Pea going out tomorrow night?"

"It sounds wonderful. What are we going to do?"

Hank winked at her. "It's a surprise."

Sadie's mouth formed a perfect bow. "Another one?"

His grin turned mischievous. "Yup. Sweet Pea and I came up with it together."

She slumped back in the chair and closed her eyes, her fatigue obvious. "If Sweet Pea is in on it, I'm sure it will be great."

Sweet Pea thumped her tail, but remained sprawled by the fire.

Hank scooted his chair closer to massage Sadie's shoulders.

She groaned. "That feels amazing."

"Your muscles are really knotted."

She nodded. "Holidays are stressful for me, and this year in particular, knowing that Jody will be leaving."

"All the more reason for an evening out."

SADIE'S DOORBELL rang at five the next evening. Hank stood on her porch, wearing a heavy parka, jeans, boots, and a Christmas hat, holding a red leash with reindeer on it. She ushered him inside, pushing her inner Grinch to the back of her mind.

Hank's gaze swept over the room. "Where's Sweet Pea?"

"With Jody. She refused to come home with me. We can pick her up on the way out."

Something akin to relief washed over him. "Oh good. She's a main part of our date tonight."

"Really? Does that mean you're ready to tell me what part Sweet Pea's playing?"

He pretended to zip his lips. "Can't say, or I'll ruin the surprise." Before she could protest further, he said, "We need to get going or we'll be late."

"Late for what?" Sadie asked as she slipped on her coat.

Hank's eyes twinkled with merriment. "You'll see soon enough."

Without another word, he escorted her out the door and down the snowy path to pick up Sweet Pea. The canine waited on the porch wearing antlers, a red collar with bells, and brown booties that looked like reindeer hooves.

They loaded into the truck, and Sadie twisted around to study the dog. "You certainly look festive."

Sweet Pea flopped her chin on Sadie's shoulder and released a pent-up sigh of contentment.

When Hank didn't respond, Sadie prodded further. "Who do you suppose dressed up Sweet Pea?"

Hank headed for downtown. "I wouldn't have a clue."

Liar, liar, pants on fire.

He knew exactly who'd dressed Sweet Pea. This had Jody's handiwork all over it. No question he'd signed Sweet Pea up for the Canine Christmas Parade. Rather than spoil Hank's surprise, she kept peppering him with questions.

"I still don't understand why it's so important that Sweet Pea joins us."

Hank flashed her a grin that told her he knew exactly what she was up to. "You're not going to get information from me, no matter how many questions you ask. This is a surprise, and I'm not giving it away."

Sweet Pea flopped her head over the front seat, her eyebrows arched as she glanced from Sadie to Hank.

Sadie patted her head to reassure her. "It's okay girl. I'm just teasing Hank to make him give up his secret."

Sweet Pea released a low grunt and stared out the windshield.

Hank cast a sidelong glance at her, his face alight with humor, then focused on the traffic as he pulled into the parking garage. They wound up three levels and pulled into an empty space.

Hank came around to open the door for Sadie, then the back door, clipping the leash to Sweet Pea. Before they set off, he held out a Christmas hat identical to his.

"This is for you."

Sadie remained motionless and, instead of accepting it, tucked her hands into her pockets. She did not dress up for the holidays.

"Come on, Grinch, be a sport and get into the holiday spirit with me, and Sweet Pea."

The dog stared up at her with adoring eyes, pleading with her to join in.

"Oh, all right." She tugged on the hat, swallowing back a bah humbug.

Hank winked at her, his hat tilted at a jaunty angle, giving him a decidedly rakish appearance. "You look adorable," he said just before he pressed a gentle kiss to her lips that made Sadie forget about the hat and the Grinch stomping around inside her.

She arched, pressing her body tightly against his, her fingers brushing the soft fur of his red hat as her arms wrapped around his neck. She wanted to stay like this in his arms, but he pulled back before she made the suggestion.

"Show time," he said and escorted her down to the street teeming with holiday shoppers, Christmas carolers, and children filled with the magic of the season.

Why couldn't she embrace the holidays like everyone else?

CHAPTER 28

December

Hank glanced down at Sadie. She really looked adorable in her hat, a wisp of hair sweeping over her forehead.

Their eyes met and her lips slightly parted. She stumbled and Hank caught her elbow. Blinking at him, she focused on her surroundings. A rumble of amusement echoed in his chest as they continued walking.

They crossed Madison Square to an alley where a horde of pet owners gathered with their dogs dressed in holiday sweaters, fancy collars, and booties. Sweet Pea barked and leapt when she saw the other dogs. She circled a border collie and a golden retriever, tails wagging, noses sniffing each other, leashes tangling around their legs. Laughter and holiday cheer filled the air and even Sadie got into the Christmas spirit, although she'd deny it if Hank pointed it out to her.

"So our date is the Reindog Parade?"

"It's part of it. You don't look that surprised."

"Well, I do keep up on the holiday activities in the city."

"And yet, according to Annie, you've never entered Sweet Pea in the parade."

"Annie has a big mouth," Sadive muttered just loud enough for him to hear, which made him laugh.

"Don't blame Annie. I asked Jack, and he asked Annie."

That seemed to appease her, but fire sparked in her eyes. "Still awfully sneaky of you."

"Sneaky is a negative term. I prefer to think of myself as clever or inventive."

"Ha! You would." Her tone amused, not angry.

Changing the subject, Hank guided her over to check-in. Once Sweet Pea had her number, Hank asked, "Is this really such a bad date?"

Sadie's sparkling laughter answered his question. "No, it's wonderful. And thank you for including Sweet Pea." She looked down at the dog whose tail had been wagging incessantly since they'd left the truck. "She loves it." She leaned in, pressing her cheek to his sleeve. "It's the perfect date."

Hank's heart thumped a happy beat against his chest.

Had he ever felt this way about Lydia?

No, he hadn't. He'd cared about Lydia, but he'd didn't have this need to know everything about her, to spend every moment with her.

A huge bell rang, then a tinny voice came over the loud-speaker. "The parade is starting in five minutes. Everyone line up, please."

He, Sadie, and Sweet Pea got in line beside the golden retriever named Sam. They chatted with Sam's owner for a moment before the parade started, then they set off.

Children, adults, teenagers cheered and waved as the dogs pranced past. Sweet Pea took in the praise as if she were a princess. The crowd patted her as she passed, and she absorbed all the attention as her due.

"Mr. D, Miss Sadie." Hank turned to see Kirstin waving frantically from her chair next to her parents. He led Sweet Pea over, and Kirstin buried her face in the dog's neck.

"Oh Sweet Pea, you look so pretty," she jabbered, then looked up at her parents. "This is Sweet Pea from Miss Sadie's farm. She gave us the tickets for movie night."

Kirstin's mother turned to Sadie. "Thank you so much for the tickets. Kirstin has talked nonstop about your farm."

A pleased blush colored Sadie's cheeks. "I'm so glad she had a good time. I loved having her and her class there."

Kirstin's mother leaned closer to Sadie, lowering her voice, "Will there be any problem getting her chair into the theater?"

"None. Hank's uncle drew the designs for the entire farm to ensure it was accessible to everyone."

Tears sparked in the woman's eyes. "I can't tell you how wonderful that is. So many times, Kristin has gotten excited about an outing only to be disappointed when her wheelchair can't be accommodated. It's a real challenge."

Sadie squeezed her hand. "Not at my farm, and if you find anything that isn't accessible, let me know so that I can address it."

The parade was moving, and they got back in line. "What a nice woman," Sadie said.

"Very nice, just like her daughter, and the dad is really great, too," Hank said.

They reached the end of the alley to find a container of biscuits shaped like Christmas cookies, from Fido and Friends, the local doggy bakery for each of the contestants.

"That was so much fun." Sadie grabbed one and offered it to Sweet Pea. She gobbled it in a single bite.

"It was," Hank agreed, "but we still have another event."

Sadie bent to pat Sweet Pea. "He is just full of surprises, isn't he, girl?"

Sweet Pea barked, and danced in a circle crashing into Sadie and sending her sprawling onto her backside. Laughing, she tried to rise, but fell back into the snow.

Hank lifted her to her feet with ease.

"Our knight in shining armor, Sweet Pea."

The dog barked in agreement, and Hank fell just a little harder for Sadie and Sweet Pea.

CHAPTER 29

Hank directed Sadie and Sweet Pea across Madison Square, decorated with blinking lights, Santa's sleigh, and a massive tree covered in ornaments. A racetrack cut through the snow with a huge Start sign at the beginning and a Finish sign next to the sleigh with eight reindeer where Jody and Nick Claws sat inside, waving to the crowd.

Sadie turned to Hank. "Did you know they'd be there?"

"This is the first I knew about it. Those two have always got something going. I'm surprised Elroy isn't here."

Sadie nodded in agreement, then pointed to a man dressed as an elf that walked up to the pair. "Isn't that your uncle?"

Hank shook his head. "It is, and why am I not surprised?"

Sadie laughed. "Elroy is involved in everything. What are we doing here?" Sadie expected more evasion from Hank, but he surprised her by telling her everything.

"It's a canine sled-pulling contest. They have dog-sized sleds they pull. The fastest in each category is the winner."

Sadie looked at the tiny sleighs, then Sweet Pea. "Are you sure she'll do this?"

Hank looked a little sheepish. "We've been practicing."

"What! When? Where?"

"At the farm. Before I'd come find you, Sweet Pea and I did test runs with the sleigh Jody put in front of the deli."

Sadie placed a hand on her hip. "How did you do this without me knowing about it?"

He dragged a boot through the snow. "Wel-l-l-l, I had some help keeping you busy while we practiced."

"Let me guess—Jody."

"And Dale, and Elroy, and Nick."

Sadie shook her head. Everyone was in on it. She rubbed Sweet Pea's ears. "So, girl, are you going to win?"

A single bark, then she danced in circles, tail wagging.

"I'll take that for a yes."

Hank captured her hand. "You don't mind, do you?"

Sadie looked from Hank to Sweet Pea. They both seemed to hang on her response. "Of course not."

Hank pressed his lips to hers. "I'm glad to hear it."

They waited behind a line of people and finally got checked in. They sipped hot chocolate while they waited. Sweet Pea would run fifth in the large dog category.

The first dog got on the start line. Sleigh bells rang, followed by a bellowing "Go!" from Nick. The owner called and encouraged his dog, but no matter how many treats he offered, it would take a few steps, stop and sit all to the amusement of the crowd. Finally, time was up, and the next dog moved to the start line.

A Great Pyrenees was next, and when Nick shouted "Go!" it took off at a slow trot, then stopped a few feet from the finish line. His owner coaxed him with treats, but he refused to pull the sled any further.

Sweet Pea's turn finally came, and she and Hank moved to the start line. Hank spoke quiet words of encouragement as they stood on the sideline. Nick shouted "Go!" and Sweet Pea took off like a shot, heading straight for the finish line with Hank running alongside her, but instead of stopping when she reached the end, she ran straight to Jody and Nick's sleigh. She skidded to a halt, dancing in circles until she tipped over the sleigh.

Hank caught up to her and unhitched the sleigh, clipped on her leash, then walked her back to Sadie, Sweet Pea prancing the entire way.

Sadie laughed at her antics with the rest of the crowd. An hour later, the event concluded and Sweet Pea took home first place. Her prize—a huge biscuit, rawhide, and a ribbon.

"What do you say we order a pizza and take it to my place so Sweet Pea can enjoy her goodies?"

Sadie slipped her arm through Hank's and pressed her cheek to his sleeve again. "Sounds perfect."

They waved goodbye to Elroy, Jody, and Nick, picked up the pizza Hank ordered on the way to the truck, then drove to his townhouse, which Sadie hadn't realized was close to Annie and Jack's house.

He escorted her inside. Ultra-modern, extremely masculine furnishings. A leather sofa and matching chair, a massive television, and a chrome-and-glass coffee table filled the small space. They headed to the miniscule kitchen and postcard-sized dining room.

Hank placed the box of pizza on the table. "Beer?" he asked as he grabbed plates from the cupboard.

"Yes, please."

He took two bottles from the fridge, then set everything on the table. Sweet Pea sat on the floor, her eyes darting back and forth between them.

"Why don't you give her the rawhide?" Hank suggested.

"Are you sure? She makes an awful mess of them."

"Of course. She earned it, and messes are part of life."

His attitude wasn't surprising, considering he dealt with

kindergarteners all day long, and chaos and disorder were part and parcel of that age group.

Another check in the keeper box.

Sadie unwrapped the rawhide and handed it to Sweet Pea, who promptly laid down, wrapped her paws around it, and started chewing.

"Thank you for tonight. I really needed a break from all the craziness that's been going on since we got back from Angel Falls."

Hank turned the pizza box her direction, and she scooped up a slice.

"It was my pleasure. And it was fun!"

"It was." Sadie bit into her pizza. "This is delicious."

Hank nodded in agreement. "Papa Lorenzo's is my favorite pizza parlor in Snowside."

"It's fantastic. So is Giovanni's."

"We'll have to go there next time."

Sadie liked that there would be another date. "Are you coming to movie night tomorrow?"

"Of course. I wouldn't miss it, and I plan to help set up."

Another check in the keeper box. The man was always ready and willing to lend a helping hand. In fact, he'd started to feel like *the one*.

Sadie shook off the notion. They'd only been dating for six weeks. How could she possibly know he was *the one*?

The heart always knows.

Her father's words rang in her head. She'd fallen for a boy a few months before her parents died. She'd told her dad she thought she was falling in love with him, but that it seemed too fast.

He'd surprised her by saying that love comes on its own timetable and that the heart knows what it wants, when it wants it.

While she'd always adhered to her father's words, they'd failed her when she married Luke. Her heart hadn't known.

Or maybe it hadn't been love.

"The kids are so excited," Hank continued, breaking into her thoughts.

"Me, too. I can't wait to see their faces when they find out we're showing *How the Grinch Stole Christmas*."

"They'll love it," Hank said. "And I'm certain they will love all the new snacks Jody created."

"How did you hear about that?"

"Nick, who else? He keeps me posted on the comings and goings at the farm."

Of course he did.

Sadie took another slice of pizza and sipped her beer, contemplating the man beside her.

"Is there anything you don't know about me?"

He took a bite of pizza and chewed before he answered. "As a matter of fact, I have a burning question I'm dying to ask."

"What's that?"

"Do you *like* me?"

CHAPTER 30

S adie's lips formed the cutest O of surprise at Hank's question. He loved throwing her off balance and leaving her at a loss for words.

She swallowed, then cleared her throat. "Of course I like you. I wouldn't be here if I didn't."

"I don't mean like as in friends, but *like* as in, I'm into you and can't keep my hands off of you."

Her smile glowed brighter than the aurora borealis and sent desire snaking through him. "I know the difference between like and *like*, and I definitely *like* you." She wiggled her eyebrows in a clearly suggestive manner that would have made Rudolph's nose glow bright red.

Hank reined in the hunger and took a slug of beer before responding. "And just for the record, I *like* you, too."

Her cheeks turned rosy, and her eyes sparked with longing when she smiled at him. He didn't know where this was going between them, but it promised a wild ride that left him eager to see what came next.

"I THINK we made some actual progress with those two tonight." Jody's gaze moved between Nick and Elroy. "What do you two think?"

Elroy swallowed the last bite of cookie. "I agree. You two have taken them from enemies to friends and the definite possibility of a permanent relationship. But am I the only one who gets the sense they're not on solid ground yet?"

Nick stroked his beard. "I would agree. It feels like they're tiptoeing around each other."

"Well, of course. They have unresolved issues they need to deal with. That's why we're here to guide them in the right direction," Jody said. Prancer raised his head from her lap and gave a single bark of agreement. "And until they are fully committed to each other, we keep nudging them together. Are we in agreement?"

A glance passed between the two men, then they nodded.

Jody clapped her hands. "Wonderful. And we have another opportunity to throw them together tomorrow night. Let's make the most of movie night."

"Do you have a plan?" Elroy asked.

Jody narrowed her gaze at him. "When have you ever known me not to have a plan?"

HANK ARRIVED at the farm after lunch the next afternoon. He'd taken the bus rather than drive and walked the two blocks to the farm. He was still flying high after the evening he'd had with Sadie and Sweet Pea, and he looked forward to spending more time with her tonight.

Entering the barn, he stepped into organized chaos with Jody at the helm, firing off orders that would have made Hank's SEAL commander proud.

Prancer and Sweet Pea stopped their play and raced over to him for pets and kisses, which he obliged.

Jody's eagle gaze zeroed in on him, and within minutes she'd put him to work—helping Sadie, which Hank realized was not by accident. But he wasn't complaining since he wanted to spend time with her.

Jody assigned him to help Sadie arrange the children's seating. He found her, grouping the chairs together. Rather than jump right into work, he caught her around the waist and took her behind the stage.

Laughing, her eyes sparkled. "We're supposed to be setting up chairs."

He drew her deeper into the shadows and leaned in, trailing kisses along her neck to her collarbone. "Later," he murmured as he nipped her earlobe and smiled when she gasped.

He pressed his lips to hers, his hands circling her waist.

She raised up on tiptoe. Wrapping her arms around his neck, she slipped her tongue inside his mouth and all he wanted was to stay right here with her—to hell with movie night.

She pulled back and pink blossomed across her cheeks. "That was the nicest hello I've had since the last time I saw you."

Hank chuckled. "I'm glad because I just had to touch you."

The pink deepened to red and her mouth formed a wordless O. Recovering, she pressed her lips to his again, and his arm drew her snug against him. When he pulled back, they were both breathing heavily.

"That was amazing," she said.

Hank rubbed his nose against hers. "Beyond amazing."

He'd been about to kiss her again when Jody's voice called out, "Who's setting up the children's seating?"

Sighing, he said, "I guess our break is over."

Sadie smiled. "I think so, and we'd better get back in there before she sends a search party after us."

Hank laughed, but more than anything, he wanted to stay right where he was with Sadie snuggled in his arms. "We will pick up where we left off later tonight."

Sadie gave him a come-hither wink. "I'm counting on it."

LAUGHTER and excited shrieks filled the barn as every child from Hank's class and their parents, and extended family filled the space. Sadie had gone home an hour ago to change into the red shirt, black pants, and vest that Jody had given her. She stared at the red and white trimmed Christmas hat and tried to still the resistance building within her.

As she stared at the sea of excited faces, she wondered why she couldn't love Christmas like everyone else. Did her DNA have a missing chromosome like her dad?

She swallowed her reluctance, put on the Christmas hat, and waited at the edge of the stage for Jody's cue to make announcements.

Hank appeared at her elbow. "Hey."

"What are you doing back here?" Sadie asked. "I thought you were sitting with the kids."

"So did I until I received new instructions from Jody."

"Which are?"

"To welcome my class, then turn the stage over to you."

As much as it felt like more of Jody's matchmaking, Sadie couldn't deny it made sense for Hank to speak to his class.

As they waited, a flutter of nerves rippled over Sadie that had more to do with the man beside her than stage fright.

Jody signaled Hank, and he stepped out on stage and held up five fingers. As the kids noticed, they shushed each other. He went to four, then three, until the room went silent.

"I'm so glad you could all make it tonight. Miss Sadie and all of her helpers," Hank gestured to the sidelines where Jody, Nick, Mickey, and a host of other volunteers stood, "have put together a really special treat for you that Miss Sadie is going to tell you about. Join me in thanking everyone who put this together with your best clapping."

Applause went up from the crowd, the loudest from the children. When it died down, Hank held out his hand to Sadie, and she stepped onto the stage, ignoring her Christmas hat tilting onto her forehead.

"Hello everyone. I'm so glad you could join us tonight." She listed off the upcoming movies for the following week, then said, "Let's get started."

Sadie moved off stage to find Hank waiting for her. Jody had provided them with a cozy sofa that they settled into. The lights dimmed, and the movie began. She couldn't help but wonder if Jody had chosen *The Grinch* with her specifically in mind.

Hank slung an arm over her shoulder, and she snuggled against him, forgetting all the reasons she avoided Christmas. Maybe this was the man who could make her embrace the holiday season, and all the magic that came with it.

CHAPTER 31

Monday morning, Hank's class was wound up tighter than a Jack-in-the-box about to pop. Between movie night at Sadie's farm and Christmas vacation just two weeks away, the kids were about to burst with excitement.

Five-year-olds, he'd learned, were the perfect age for the holidays, and Santa Claus in particular. Their excitement level ratcheted up as each day took them closer to Christmas and having their very own Saint Nick in the classroom kept them in a state of perpetual stimulation.

Every day, one or more of the kids whispered excitedly to Nick what they wanted for Christmas, and Nick took it all in stride, making careful notes on a roll of parchment he kept with him at all times.

It seemed to Hank that his beard grew longer with each passing day, too, and his belly broader. He didn't know if it was possible, but Nick's eyes twinkled brighter, and his laughter echoed more robustly.

What would he do when Nick left after the holidays?

The kids would be devastated, but hopefully he could

convince him to come back after the break just so the kids could say goodbye.

"Mr. D.! Mr. D.!" Kirstin called out, her hand waving impatiently.

Hank nodded at Kirstin.

"I want to show you my Christmas tree," she said, her smile as wide and bright as the sunshine streaming in the window.

Hank made his way over to see her latest creation. Kirstin spared no color of the rainbow. He reached her table and looked down at her Christmas tree drawn in dark blue with red dots scattered over it.

"Tell me about your tree."

"Well, this is our Christmas tree." She pointed to the dark skeleton of a tree on the page, "and these are my ornaments." She touched the one up high on the tree. "This is my favorite. Mama puts it way at the top of the tree so it doesn't get knocked off and broken. It's a flying Christmas angel that's made of glass, and painted all in red."

"I see presents under the tree. Who are they for?" Hank asked.

"This one's Mama's, and this one's Daddy's, and the rest are mine."

"Who gave your mom and dad presents?"

Kirstin jabbed her chest. "They're from me!"

"What did you get them?"

Kirstin leaned in close and lowered her voice to a stage whisper. "It's a secret. I'm not supposed to tell anyone."

Hank hid a grin and said, "I won't tell anyone."

"You swear?"

He crossed his heart.

Kirstin stared up at him. "Just make sure you don't tell Mommy and Daddy."

At his nod, she continued, "I drew pictures for them."

"They will love them."

Kirstin's smile stayed with him as he went to the front of the room while she drew another picture.

He leaned a hip on the corner of his desk, surveying the classroom. He'd made the right decision coming to Snowside. While he missed his family, he had a job he loved.

If only he had someone to share that life with.

An image of Sadie rose to his mind, reminding him he wasn't alone. He had Sadie.

AFTER THE KIDS left for the day, Hank cleaned the classroom. He was just about finished when Nick came in with hot cocoa and cookies—his usual fare.

"Thought you might need a pick me up," Nick said.

"That sounds perfect. Thank you." Hank pulled an extra chair up to his desk while Nick set everything down, handing him a cup of cocoa.

"Is something bothering you?" Nick asked.

Hank selected a cookie as he contemplated Nick's question. He supposed he should be upset since Lydia had broken their engagement a little over a year ago, but he wasn't.

"Your broken heart is healing," Nick observed.

Hank studied the other man closely, trying to determine if there might be something otherworldly going on here—like Nick actually was Santa Claus and knew his deepest thoughts and desires.

Hank shook off the whimsy, telling himself he'd spent too much time in the company of kindergarteners. He knew Santa was a fictional character, but if he were honest, deep down, he wanted to believe.

Nick interrupted his musings. "Jody and I always find the

holidays the most joyous of times for us, but we never forget that isn't the case for everyone."

"As I'm sure you've seen, a lot of my students don't have the best home environment and many times the holidays just aren't magical for them. That's why I try to keep everything upbeat for them."

Nick nodded. "I've seen it. Jody and I do everything in our power to bring joy to everyone during the holidays. We never want to see any child unhappy."

"The best Christmas I could ever have is knowing that every single one of my kids felt loved and cherished."

Nick's expression turned somber. "That's a tall order, but I'd like to see that myself."

Hank selected another cookie, and pondered what he could do to accomplish that goal. "Any suggestions on how I might achieve that?"

Nick sipped his cocoa as he considered Hank's question. "I think perhaps we need expert advice on this."

Hank grinned. "Expert, as in Jody?"

"The one and only."

"Is she ever at a loss for ideas?"

Nick picked up a cookie. "Never. She always has something up her sleeve."

Hank had seen that firsthand, and it was a trait he appreciated about her. Neither she or Nick seemed in short supply of energy, ideas, and passion for ensuring everyone's happiness. This pair was a wonder, and if anyone could bring joy to the holidays, it was them.

CHAPTER 32

S adie worked on berry preserves for the store, pouring the cooked fruit into jars. They'd already sold out what she'd made the week before, and since she'd had a bumper crop this year, and froze the excess in the fall, she used them to make more jam.

She'd just started the second batch when Jody came in with Prancer and Sweet Pea trailing after her. The two curled up on Sweet Pea's bed and went to sleep.

"The last group just left. Could you use some help?" Jody asked.

Gratitude filled her. It was so much easier with an extra pair of hands. "Thank you. I can't tell you how much I appreciate it."

Jody waved aside her thanks. "No worries. I love cooking."

So far as Sadie could tell, Jody loved everything. "Is there anything you don't enjoy doing?"

Her question produced a chuckle. "Well, if you put me at a desk in an office with no windows and nobody to chat with, I would not be a happy camper."

No question, Jody was a people person through and through. "Well, I'm grateful for your help, and I agree, being around people is much better than being stuck in an office, and so much more fun."

Jody tied on an apron, then scrubbed her hands and dug right in without needing to be told what to do.

"Have you heard anything from Congresswoman Menudo?" Jody asked.

She'd told Jody about her appointment with the congresswoman since she'd had to be gone, but she'd sworn her to secrecy, as she didn't want anyone else to know. "Nothing yet, but that reminds me I need to call her and check in. I'm not holding my breath that anything will come of this."

"Of course it will. You just need to have faith and believe in the magic of Christmas."

Jody's answer to everything—just believe in Christmas magic. Sadie tamped down a bah humbug since magic didn't exist, especially Christmas magic. With as many times as they'd turned down her application, she refused to get her hopes up, only to have them dashed again.

She changed the subject. "How did the craft class go?"

Jody gave her a long stare that told her she knew a diversion when she saw it. Thankfully, she went along with it. "Exceptionally well."

"This was the senior ladies' day, wasn't it?"

"Yes, and those ladies are incredibly talented. They came up with some amazing ideas I intend to incorporate into our next class."

"Like what?" Sadie asked.

"Well, we made the most beautiful snowflakes out of tie-dyed coffee filters.

"Coffee filters? I would have never thought of using something like that."

"The group was thrilled when I told them I was going to display them in the front window. This class just keeps growing every week. I may have to expand to two classes a week to keep up."

Sadie added sugar to the bubbling pot of berries and stirred. What was she going to do when Jody left? There is no way she could manage all these classes, but she kept postponing advertising for her replacement.

Jody's hand squeezed hers. "What's wrong?"

Sadie slanted her gaze to the older woman. There was no point brushing off her question because Jody being Jody, would only persist. "You've done such a fabulous job." Sadie's shoulders slumped as if the weight of the world rested on her, which she wasn't so sure it didn't. "I don't know what to do. I don't think I can find anyone to replace you."

Jody patted her hand. "Don't you worry about a thing. I'm working on that, and I'm not going anywhere until I know you have the perfect replacement."

Sadie wondered if Jody was a miracle worker, because every time she had a problem, Jody found a solution, or so it seemed.

"Thank you. You always know just the right words to ease my mind."

Jody hugged her, and the scent of cinnamon and cloves filled Sadie's senses as it always did whenever she got close to the other woman and a sense of contentment settled over her. Maybe everything would work out.

CHAPTER 33

Sadie came back from feeding the animals Sunday morning to help with the *No Grinches Allowed Brunch*.

Had Jody indirectly chosen that title to goad her?

Entirely possible. Sadie thought she'd kept her inner Grinch in line, but maybe she wasn't as skilled as she'd thought.

Jody called out to her, and she focused on the getting everything together for the brunch. Jody had a list of activities from Christmas Bingo to Holiday Charades for attendees. The moment Jody put out the announcement for the event, customers had scrambled to buy tickets.

She crossed the room. "What do you need?"

"Someone in the kitchen to help Nick and Elroy with the meal preparation."

"I'm on it."

When she'd told Sadie about the brunch, Sadie had been skeptical they could pull it off. Where would they get the servers, the cooks—but Jody had silenced her with a look and assured her she had it under control. And she had. Everything was running smoothly, including the servers, which Jody had gotten from the local high school—kids in need of service credits for their college applications. Why hadn't she thought of that?

She went to the kitchen and found herself thrust into organized chaos for the next hour as they prepared dozens of French toast casseroles. Sadie's job—icing the cinnamon rolls as they came out of the oven. Applesauce pancakes scented the air as Nick began pouring batter onto the grill.

Sadie's stomach rumbled as all the delicious scents filled the kitchen.

Jody popped in, and she clapped her hands, rousing the dogs from sleep. "It's time. The servers are here and ready to put the food out. Tell me it's ready."

Nick's laughter filled the room. "When have I ever let you down?"

"Never, but there's always a first time."

Nick expertly flipped the trio of pancakes on the grill, then tugged Jody into his arms and kissed her, making her already pink cheeks shine brighter. "Send in the servers."

Jody gave him a hard squeeze. "I can always count on you," she said, then stepped away.

A tug of longing settled over Sadie. She wanted what Nick and Jody had. As if on cue, Hank entered, his gaze searching the room. When it settled on her, warmth seeped into her and his grin put a hitch in her breath as he made a beeline for her. Suddenly, everything felt right in Sadie's world.

"Did you come for brunch?" she asked.

Hank shook his head. "I came for you."

He knew just the right words to make her feel like she was important and special to him. She squeezed his arm. "You always know the perfect thing to say. How do you do that?"

His eyes darkened, sending a shiver of desire through her. "I speak the truth as I see it."

Those words replayed in her head as the morning flew past

with food preparation, serving, and clean up. When the last customer left, all the volunteers sank down at the empty tables, Hank collapsing into the chair beside her.

Sadie's stomach rumbled, but before she could find the energy to fill a plate, the servers from the high school materialized carrying heaping platters of food—fresh baked cinnamon rolls, fluffy applesauce pancakes with fresh maple syrup, and French toast casserole.

Sadie's gaze circled the room until she found Jody busily directing the servers. She should have known Jody was behind it. The woman didn't miss a thing.

With a weary smile, Sadie thanked the teenager for the mug of steaming coffee and sipped. The surge of caffeine rejuvenated her as she waited for Hank to finish filling his plate, then she accepted the platter from him, and loaded hers.

She bit into the cinnamon roll, the icing dripping onto her plate. "OMG, this is amazing."

Hank nodded in agreement.

The high school kids finished setting out the food and joined in to eat their fill. Jody made the rounds, checking to see that everyone had plenty to eat and drink until Sadie insisted she sit down and relax.

Taking the chair directly across from her, Jody filled a plate and dug in.

"So, how did the brunch go? Do you think it was a success?" Sadie asked.

Prancer hopped onto Jody's lap, and she offered him a piece of her pancake. "I thought it went great. What did you think?"

Sadie shrugged. "I was in the kitchen. I didn't really get to see the event, but I heard lots of laughter, which I took as a good sign."

"Oh, I forgot you were behind the scenes. People raved about the food. I skimmed through the comment box, and the ones I read were all positive. And for those who took part, the Christmas bingo was a huge success. I think most everyone donated their winnings to Job Hunters 4 You."

"That's wonderful. I can't thank you enough for doing this." She turned to all the volunteers. "Thanks all of you for your time and effort. It means more than I can say."

Plenty of smiles, and you're welcomes, and happy-to-do-it's circulated the room. These people were family to her. How would she ever repay them for all they'd done?

HANK CLEANED his plate and pushed it aside to sip his coffee. A chin flopped on his thigh, and he looked down to see Sweet Pea staring up at him. He rubbed her ears, and her tongue lolled out the side of her mouth.

"You've made a friend," Sadie said, reaching over to scrape her nails along the dog's jaw.

"It appears so. What are you two doing this afternoon?"

"Absolutely nothing except plugging in a movie and chilling."

"Would you mind some company?"

Sadie's gaze slid over him. "So long as you're the company, we'd love it."

Hank grinned. "Great." A snowy afternoon, a movie, and Sadie's lush body to snuggle with sounded like the perfect Sunday afternoon.

When everyone finished eating, they cleared away the plates, put the food away, and everyone said their goodbyes, then Sadie and Hank, with Sweet Pea loping ahead through the fresh snow, took the path to her house.

The fire had died down, so while Sadie grabbed some blankets, Hank added wood to the fire. Within minutes, it was popping and crackling.

Sadie made them hot toddies, and they settled onto the sofa, scrolling through the movie options until she came to a new action/adventure film. "What do you think?" she asked Hank.

"I thought you'd choose a Christmas movie."

She shrugged. "It doesn't matter to me, but if you want a holiday movie, I'm fine with that." She offered him the remote, and he clicked on *It's a Wonderful Life*.

Sadie didn't object, but Hank sensed it wouldn't have been her first choice. She curled up beside him as the whimsical Christmas movie played.

Her soft, even breathing echoed over him as ZuZu Bailey said, "Look, Daddy, teacher says, every time a bell rings, an angel gets his wings."

Hank brushed his knuckles over her cheek, then pressed a kiss to her forehead.

She burrowed deeper against him, and everything felt right with the world as he settled back to watch the movie, Sadie tucked against his side.

CHAPTER 34

Hank gazed down at Sadie, her head nestled against his chest, her soft breaths punctuated with an occasional sigh. There was no point in denying the truth any longer. He loved her, but he wasn't certain the feelings were reciprocated. She'd told him about her divorce with the briefest of explanations, and he suspected it had something to do with her hesitancy to move forward in their relationship. He had to find a way to break through her fears and convince her she could trust him.

Leaning back against the cushions, he stretched his legs onto the coffee table to watch the movie, but didn't make it any further than the car crash before he dozed off. A low whine woke him an hour later. Sweet Pea's head on his thigh, the dog blew out a breath, ruffling Sadie's hair.

"What's wrong, girl?" he asked softly.

She released another pent-up whine, gazing up at Hank as if he should be able to read her mind. She nudged his elbow, then moved to the door.

Message loud and clear—*I need out.*

Hank eased out from under Sadie, gently placing her head on the sofa, then crossed over to open the door. Sweet Pea rushed out, did her business, shook off the snow and came back in the house, dropping onto her bed next to the dwindling fire. Hank added more wood, then lifted Sadie so she leaned against him. He pulled a blanket over them, and settled in to watch the rest of the movie.

The credits were rolling when Sadie shifted and her eyes slowly opened. "What time is it?" she asked, suppressing a yawn.

"Almost five."

She stretched her arms overhead. "Wow, I never take naps."

Hank traced a finger over her lips, his mouth following.

"Mmmmm."

When he pulled back, her eyes were dark as emeralds. "I could use something warm to drink. How about you?" he asked.

She blinked as if coming out of a daze. "Uh, sure. What would you like?"

She started to rise, but he stopped her. "I'll get it. You stay here. How does another hot toddy sound?"

"Delicious," she said.

"I'll be right back." He fixed their drinks and carried them back to the living room. She'd shut off the television and sat huddled under the blanket. The power flickered, then went out so that the only light came from the fire.

Hank set the mug down and added more wood to the fire before joining her. They sipped their drinks in comfortable silence.

Sadie turned, sitting cross-legged as she faced him. "What is it you want to discuss?"

Hank twirled his glass, watching the coppery liquid swirl around before raising his eyes to meet hers. "I never said I wanted to talk."

Sadie's smile softened her face. "You didn't have to. You have a tell."

"I do not."

"Do, too."

"What is it?"

She shook her head, her hair swaying softly from side to side. "Not saying. I might need it if we play poker someday." She waited a beat, then said, "What's on your mind?"

"Us."

"What about us?"

He sipped his drink, then set it down and looked her directly in the eye. "I have feelings for you. I want more than just casual dating."

Her eyes went wide. "Aren't we exclusive, or did I misread what's going on between us?"

"That's just it. I assumed we were, but we've never discussed it, and I want to be sure that I make my intentions clear."

She gripped her drink. "So, you want us to be exclusive, too?"

The uncertainty in her voice sent a wave of protectiveness through him. He threaded his fingers through hers. "Yes, that's what I want with all my heart."

Her expression brightened. "Good, then we're on the same page."

Hank nodded. "We are."

She released a breath, and asked, "So you're over Lydia?"

He blinked at the sudden change in subject. "Yes, absolutely."

"It didn't feel that way to me at the mini mart."

Lydia had broken his heart and stolen his trust, but he'd moved on. "I'm over her."

"If that's the case, then why all the tension between you two?"

Hank exhaled a long breath. "Lydia and I have a long history. We grew up together, but we didn't start dating until I was discharged. I missed the camaraderie of the military, and she filled the loneliness inside me.

"I was done with military life, but didn't know what I wanted to do next. Lydia knew exactly what she wanted. She planned to use me and my family to help build her career as a Realtor."

"What does that mean?"

Hank's gut tightened remembering the call from his mom that icy November morning when she'd told him what Lydia was up to. "It means she tried to pressure Mom into selling the family pub to her under market value."

Sadie gasped. "That's horrible. She didn't get away with it, did she?"

Hank shook his head. "Mom told me what was going on before she could, and I reported her to the Association of Realtors."

"What a terrible thing to do to your future mother-in-law." Sadie paused for a moment, then asked, "Is that why you accused me of trying to steal Elroy's property?"

Hank nodded. "It wasn't my finest hour. It was obvious to anyone with a brain that you weren't trying to do that. I was still so angry at Lydia, I instantly thought the worst."

"I would have reacted the same way." She trailed her fingers across his jaw. "I'm sorry she did that to you. It's hard when someone you love betrays your trust."

He stared into eyes wondering how her ex had hurt her. "What did Luke do to you?"

She went still, then waved a hand. "That's ancient history."

He traced a finger over the slope of her ear. "Maybe so, but I'd still like to know."

She was silent for so long, he started to wonder if she would tell him. Finally, she said, "We had a whirlwind romance and married a few months after we met. Unfortunately, our attraction didn't translate into the kind of love that you build a marriage on.

I should have seen it, but I was lonely and saw what I wanted to see." She pushed to her feet. "How about some dinner?"

Without waiting for his response, she headed to the kitchen.

Hank stared after her. She'd given him the bare bones version of her breakup—again. Would she ever trust him enough to tell him the whole story?

CHAPTER 35

Annie stopped by the farm Monday, and she and Sadie had lunch in the back room, away from customers and prying eyes. They opened their sandwiches, and Sadie took a healthy bite as Annie tore open her bag of chips and ate one, her eyes never leaving Sadie.

"Okay, what's the real reason you're here?" Sadie asked.

Annie shrugged. "Can't friends have lunch together?"

They could, but Annie had a purpose behind her visit, which most likely meant prying into her relationship with Hank. "Definitely, but you're here for more than lunch."

Annie fluttered her lashes at her. "Shoot me for living vicariously through you. There's something special about a new romance, so this old, married, pregnant lady wants details."

Sadie couldn't help but laugh. "Okay, here's the latest—we are exclusive."

Annie rolled her eyes. "Old news. You two have been exclusive since your first date."

That was probably true. "Well, we said it out loud Saturday night."

Annie huffed out a breath. "Tell me you two did more than that."

A flush stained Sadie's cheeks. To date, their relationship hadn't moved beyond the PG stage because she kept putting the brakes on. But she couldn't deny they'd been dating almost two months and most couples would have moved beyond kissing at this point.

Would Hank get tired of waiting for her?

Annie's hand squeezed hers. "What's wrong?"

Sadie thought over the conversation she'd had Hank Saturday night when he'd told her all about Lydia, and she'd given him another diluted version of her breakup with Luke.

"He told me about his breakup with Lydia." She glanced at the open door as Jody passed by, headed for her class.

"Maybe we should have gone to the house," Annie said.

Sadie shrugged. "It doesn't matter. Jody finds out everything eventually." Besides, she didn't have time to waste going to the house, so the back room would have to suffice.

"Am I going to have to pry the info out of you, or are you going to cut to the chase and tell me what's upsetting you?"

Tears rushed to Sadie's eyes, and she swallowed back the lump forming in her throat before offering her friend a crooked smile. "He asked me about my breakup with Luke."

"Did you tell him?"

"Sort of."

"What does that mean?"

Sadie toyed with a chip. "I told him we had a whirlwind romance, but it wasn't enough to sustain a marriage."

"You didn't tell him about Luke cheating on you?"

Sadie shook her head. "I couldn't," she whispered.

"It wasn't your fault."

Annie was a true blue friend, but she didn't know about the things Luke said to her. No one did.

Sadie gripped her glass of water, staring out the window as Sweet Pea raced past with Prancer chasing after her, the two running in circles, kicking up snow. Oh, to be so carefree, but life wasn't like that. It was filled with heartache and loss, something she never forgot, especially during the holidays.

"Relationships don't fare very well unless you can share your most intimate thoughts and feelings. Any fool can see Hank isn't Luke. He loves you and you can trust him." Annie watched her closely. "Is it possible you're looking for an excuse not to tell him the truth about Luke?"

Was she? There was no question her divorce had left deep scars, so, yes, she was being cautious and protecting her heart.

"I see I've given you something to think about. If you keep on this path, you risk missing out on love for fear of being hurt."

Annie's words resonated deep inside. Maybe she was right. Until she told Hank everything, they didn't stand a chance.

Annie pushed to her feet and hugged her. "I need to pick up Zoe. Thanks for lunch."

"You barely touched your food."

"I know. I fill up fast, but in twenty minutes I'll be starving, so I'll finish it later." She wrapped up the sandwich and tucked it into the bag, along with her chips.

Sadie walked her out to her car, shivering as the icy wind sliced through her. She hugged Annie goodbye, then watched her drive away.

Was Annie right? If she wanted the kind of close relationship Annie had with Jack, did she have to open up to Hank about her past?

HANK HAD JUST FINISHED SHOWERING after his workout Sunday afternoon, his hair still damp when the doorbell rang. He grabbed a towel and wiped his forehead, then tossed it around his neck as he went to answer the door. His pulse sped up when he found Sadie on his doorstep, a hesitant smile on her on her lips as if unsure of her welcome, Sweet Pea at her side.

He smiled and drew her into his arms, ignoring the cold air that sent a chill over him and kissed her as if he hadn't seen her in weeks when it had only been the night before.

He pulled back and her breath fogged when she said, "Oh my."

He grinned, his ego stroked with her reaction and ushered them inside. "Coffee?"

"Y-Y-Yes, I'd love some."

He helped her out of her coat and paused to admire the snug-fitting sweater before he led her into the kitchen. She sat down at the table as he reached into the cupboard and took out two mugs. Speaking over his shoulder, he asked, "What brings you by?" He passed her a cup of steaming coffee, then set out the cream and sugar before taking the chair next to her.

Sadie added sugar and stirred, clearly stalling. Finally, she raised her gaze to his. "I, um, wanted to…" Her voice trailed off, and she clutched her mug.

Hank gently prodded her. "You wanted to what?"

She swallowed before momentarily looking away.

Hank laid a hand over hers and waited for her to look at him. When she did, he said, "You can tell me anything."

She flashed him a nervous smile and said, "I know." She bit into her lower lip. "Sweet Pea and I were going for a walk and we were hoping you'd join us."

Her cheeks flushed, and Hank was certain that wasn't the reason for her visit. Sweet Pea dropped her head on his thigh, releasing a low, empathetic whine as if begging him to accept her excuse. He rubbed her ears, and she released another pitiful sigh, her dark eyes staring up at them, making Hank smile.

Rather than press Sadie, he said, "Dogs certainly know how to make their feelings known, don't they?"

The breath whooshed out of her and she relaxed. "They do. So, what about the walk?"

Sweet Pea sprang to life, circling and barking.

Hank laughed. "I'd say that's a yes from Sweet Pea and me."

Sadie's relief was palpable. Hank wished she'd tell him what was on her mind, but instead gave her the space to confide in him when she was ready.

They rose, pulled on their coats, and Sadie clipped on Sweet Pea's leash, then they set off, the snow falling softly around them.

They took the path that led them into a nearby neighborhood.

"These folks really deck the halls," Hank said, gesturing to the house covered in lights.

Sadie burst out laughing. "A tactful way of saying they overdid it a little."

Hank studied the hundreds and hundreds of twinkling Christmas lights, huge inflatable decorations of Frosty, Santa's workshop, and Yoda wearing a Christmas hat, clutching a candy cane, and said, "That wasn't what I was thinking at all. Actually, I love it, and I'm sure every kid in the neighborhood comes by to see it."

"I'll bet they get a lot of looky-loos, too." She leaned in close and whispered, "Don't you think it looks a lot like the house on *Christmas Vacation*?"

Hank laughed. "It does." As they climbed a hill, a curse, then a shout echoed over the neighborhood where a man adjusted Christmas lights, while his wife directed him.

"More to the right, Barney."

"What's wrong with where they are?""They're crooked."

"So?"

"So, have some pride in our home, why don't you?"

He muttered something unintelligible, then moved the ladder

and adjusted the lights. "Better?" Sarcasm oozed from him that didn't escape his wife's notice.

"I don't see why you're so cranky. It's Christmas. Don't you want to do this for the kids?"

"Our kids aren't even coming home, so what difference does it make?"

Sadness passed over her face. "I know, but it's still nice to have it decorated for the neighborhood kids."

"They don't give a damn about whether or not the lights are straight."

They continued on, the couple's bickering echoing after them as they turned onto the next block. Sadie's soft laughter made him smile.

"What's funny?" he asked.

"That couple. It reminds me of my parents. They used to squabble like that every year. Dad hated putting up Christmas decorations and would become a total bear. Mom took it all in stride and would gently remind him I was watching. He'd try to hide his annoyance, but I knew it wasn't directed at me. He just hated putting up decorations."

"Did it upset you?"

Sadie shook her head. "No, Mom and I would tease Dad that he had the Grinch gene, and it became the family joke."

"Sounds nice."

She was silent a moment, then nodded, her smile bittersweet. "It's a pleasant memory."

They walked on in companionable silence, Sweet Pea prancing along in front of them. Turning another corner, they came upon a snowman competition with kids and adults participating.

Hank squeezed Sadie's hand. "Let's build a snowman."

Her smile was brighter than any of the Christmas lights they'd passed. She tugged him forward to where a pair of teenagers were building a monstrous snowman. "Can anyone join in?" she asked.

"Sure. Mrs. Hall started it, and she's got all kinds of things set out to decorate them." He pointed to a house three doors down.

Within minutes, they had their own snowman underway with Sweet Pea joining in the fun.

"I think we should do something unique," Sadie said.

"Like what?"

Scrolling through her phone, she showed him a picture. "What do you think of this?"

Hank looked at the photo and started laughing. "I love it!"

They quickly put their snowman together, rolling balls of snow for the body. They were one of the last to finish, having joined in late.

Sadie stood back and studied their snowman, grinning. "If this competition gets heated, our snowman is sunk."

"He does have his head buried in the snow, doesn't he?"

Sadie went from a snicker to a full out belly laugh. "He does, but I like him that way. It gives him character."

"Hey, look at this one," someone shouted.

A little boy ran over to Hank and Sadie's snowman. "Look, Mommy, the snowman is standing on his head."

Several people came over to look at their creation, laughing and pointing at their upside-down snowman.

"I think your snowman's dancing on the ceiling," the teenager they'd spoken to originally teased.

"Looks like the wind sent him head over heels," someone else chimed in.

"Sure hope he doesn't get a bad head cold," said another.

"Or a brain freeze," another teenager said.

"Looks like he's head over heels for love at first frost," Hank fired back.

More puns followed until Sadie and Hank were in fits of laughter as they bid their goodbyes and headed home with Sweet Pea in the lead.

CHAPTER 36

Nine days to Christmas

Hank poured a cup of coffee Thursday morning and had just taken a sip when his phone rang. His mother's name scrolled across the screen. "Hey Mom, what's up?"

"Nothing special. Just hadn't talked in a while and I wanted to see how things are going."

"Things are good here. What about you? What's going on in Angel Falls?"

"Well, I'm staying busy with all the family here, but I sure miss having you around."

Guilt stabbed him. "I know. I miss you, too, and I'm sorry I haven't been back since Thanksgiving. Work has kept me too busy to get away."

His mother's voice turned sly. "I'm sure Sadie's keeping you occupied, too. Am I wrong?"

She wasn't, but then she seldom was. "If you're asking how it's going with Sadie, the answer is good."

"And?"

"And what?" Hank asked. He couldn't keep from teasing her just a little.

"And you're not going to let her slip away, are you?"

"If that's your way of asking if I'm serious about her, the answer is that we're dating exclusively, but beyond that, I don't know."

"Someone's a little huffy."

Hank released the breath he didn't realize he'd been holding. "I'm sorry, Mom. I'm a little touchy because I don't want to mess this up with Sadie. I'm trying not to push her."

A long silence followed that his mother broke. "Lydia called me yesterday."

A tidal wave of anger surged through him. "Why is she calling you? I told her not to contact you again."

"Calm down. She wasn't pressuring me to sell."

"Then what did she want?"

"She wants to talk to you."

Hank stared out the kitchen window at the cluster of low-lying clouds gathering on the horizon. "About what?" He didn't have anything to say to her, and he'd have thought that not answering her messages would have been a clue. The last thing he wanted was to talk to her since the mention of her name only got him fired up.

"She didn't say. She just left a number. Maybe she wants to apologize."

Hank snorted. "That seems out of character for her."

Another lengthy silence, and he felt his mother's censure as if she were standing next to him. "Have you considered hearing her out might allow you to move on?"

He bit down on the sharp response. "I'm over her."

"I know you don't have romantic feelings for her, but you certainly have a lot of resentment."

"Do you think if I sit down and talk to Lydia, I'll stop being angry she tried to cheat you?"

"I wish I knew, but maybe you need to think about what upsets you so much about her."

Hank considered her comment. "Okay, Mom, text me the number, and I'll handle it. Talk to you soon. Love you."

"Love you, too."

Hank disconnected the call. Maybe it was time he sat down with Lydia to see what she had to say. He'd told Sadie everything about his breakup with Lydia, but until he got rid of the fury burning in his gut, he'd never be completely free of his ex.

JODY HAD COOKIES, hot chocolate, and spiced cider set out in preparation for the next group of crafters due in thirty minutes. Nick and Elroy showed up ten minutes later, and she took them to the back room.

She handed them each a mug of hot chocolate, then pushed the plate of cookies in front of them. "Okay, give me details on your progress," she said to the men.

Elroy accepted the cocoa, and launched into his update. "Well, I have to say I've never seen Hank so happy. These two just click, but—"

Jody cut a sharp look at Elroy. "But what?"

Elroy fiddled with his napkin. "But Hank's not sure she's committed to him."

Jody dabbed a napkin to her lips. "Is he still afraid Sadie will hurt him like Lydia did? Surely he must see that Sadie would never do that."

"No, I don't think that's the problem."

"Then what is it?" Jody asked.

Elroy nibbled on his cookie as he thought over her question.

"It's Sadie. Her ex-husband said cruel things to her. She's never told me what exactly, but I know it destroyed her trust in men."

Jody scrunched her nose as she considered his comment. "Okay, so how do we help Sadie trust again?"

Both men were silent as they chewed their cookies. Elroy wiped his mouth, and said, "I suppose the best way is to encourage Sadie to tell Hank what happened."

"And if that doesn't work?" Nick asked.

Jody tapped her nails on the table as she thought over the problem, "Maybe we visit her dreams and show her the future without Hank."

Elroy nodded. "That could work. Let her see what she could lose if she keeps playing it safe."

"That's a dandy idea," Nick agreed. "And in the meantime, I'll continue to push Hank," he glanced at his wife, "nudge him," he amended, "to keep asking Sadie for more information."

Voices echoed from the front. Jody glanced at the clock. "My next class is here." She offered Nick and Elroy another cookie before they headed out. She caught Nick's arm before he left. "You are making opportunities to point out how perfect Hank and Sadie are together, aren't you?"

Nick's eyes twinkled with the devil. "Of course. I've been at this long enough to know your expectations." He leaned in and pecked Jody's cheek, then waved goodbye and headed out the door.

THE BARN DOOR OPENED, and Sadie expected to see Hank, but was delighted when Elroy made his way to the back. Refilling the water dish for the rabbits, she turned and hugged him. "What are you doing here?"

He held up the cookie. "Stealing cookies."

Sadie smiled. "There's no shortage of Christmas cookies around here these days."

Elroy handed her a napkin. She opened it to find a Christmas tree artfully decorated with blue icing and tiny silver ornaments. "This is just what I needed. Thank you." Sadie gestured to the battered chairs in the corner, and they sat down. "Besides pilfering cookies, what brings you by?"

"I can't get anything past you, can I?"

"Absolutely not. So spill. What are you doing here?"

Elroy's expression turned serious. "I wanted to find out if you had any luck on the financing."

Sadie's heart sank. Had he decided to sell to someone else? "Not yet. I talked to Congresswoman Menudo, and she's supposed to be working on it, but I haven't heard anything."

"Don't look so stricken. I have no intention of selling it out from under you. I just wanted to see if you'd made any progress."

Sadie drew in a deep breath and blew it out, the tension flowing from her. She'd thought Elroy had received an offer for the property. "Sorry. I've been tense with no word about the funding, but it seems only reasonable I wouldn't hear anything until after the holidays."

"Bull pucky."

"What does that mean?"

"It means I don't see you shutting down for the holidays. The federal government is still open. Don't wait."

What he said made sense, but still she hesitated. A lot of corporations slowed down around the holidays, but she wasn't certain about government offices. "It's only been a few weeks," she hedged.

Sadie said it like that explained everything, but the truth was, if she didn't call, she wouldn't have to hear she'd been rejected —again.

"There's a fine line between giving them time and letting them forget about you," Elroy grumbled.

He wasn't wrong. "All right, I'll call tomorrow morning."

Elroy gave a satisfied grunt, then shook a finger at her. "And don't be sweet, kind Sadie. Be the Sadie with a titanium spine. Don't take no for an answer or any other lame excuse."

Sadie couldn't prevent the smile from forming. Elroy could be cantankerous when the situation called for it, but deep down beat a heart of pure gold. "Thank you for the pep talk. I needed it."

"It's what I'm here for."

Elroy waved goodbye, and Sadie went back to feeding the animals. Lunchtime had come and gone by the time she finally took a break and traipsed through the snow for food.

Jody's class had just let out as Sadie headed to the bathroom to wash up. The deli had closed, so she went to the kitchen, made a salad, and warmed up the soup of the day. The microwave dinged. Setting the soup on a tray next to the salad and a slice of toasted French bread, she took it out front.

She'd just settled into her chair when Jody entered, Prancer and Sweet Pea on her heels. Jody took the seat opposite her, a cup of coffee cradled in her hands. "You're having a late lunch."

Sadie heard the scolding tone behind her words. "Elroy came to see me, and I got behind, and then there's a new batch of kittens I was cuddling. I just lost track of the time."

"I never lose track of meals," Jody said.

Her words made Sadie smile. She couldn't picture Jody losing track of anything. She was the most organized person she'd ever met.

"What was Elroy looking for?" Jody asked.

Sadie munched on her salad as she recalled their conversation. "Giving me the what for, for being too nice."

Jody's laughter washed over her. "That sounds like Elroy. Was it anything specific?"

Sadie nodded. "He wants me to get a status report from the congresswoman about the loan."

"And he's absolutely right. You need to keep at them. There are so many people asking for assistance, it's easy to get lost in the shuffle."

Sadie forked up a bite of salad. "So I've been told. How did class go this morning?"

Jody waved her hands, glittery red nails sparkling in the low light. "We made the cutest candy cane wreaths. You're going to have to check them out after you finish eating."

Sadie promised her she would. "Do you have any other classes coming up?

"Oh yes, I've got a whole series of classes using pinecones and more bow tying classes. They are my most popular."

"I can't wait to see the wreaths." Sadie touched her hand. "I don't know how to thank you for all you've done. I could never have managed the classes, or the events, and kept up with the farm without you. Thank you."

Jody squeezed her fingers in return. "It's been my pleasure. I love doing this, so thank you for allowing me to do what I love."

"I'm really going to miss you when you leave."

Jody patted her hand. "I'm going to miss you, too. This has been one of the best volunteer sessions I've ever had, and we do them every single year."

What would she do when Jody left?

CHAPTER 37

Sadie trudged back to the house two nights later with Sweet Pea loping along in front of her, bounding into snow drifts, then shaking off the snow. Sadie laughed at her antics as she climbed the porch steps.

Since Hank played basketball with Mickey and Jack on Thursday nights, she wouldn't have dinner with him, so she heated up leftovers, then filled the tub with steaming water and slid into it. The warm water soothed her aching muscles as she settled back against the rim.

It had been a long day of harvesting lettuce, helping Dale with the deli and Jody with prep for the carnival.

Her last thoughts were of Hank before her eyes drifted closed, the water lapping over her achy muscles.

"WAKE UP, SLEEPY HEAD."

Someone shook her shoulder, but she ignored it.

"Sadie!"

Her eyes opened to see Jody beside her, but instead of soaking in the bathtub, she wore flannel pajamas.

Jody held out her parka. "Put this on. It's chilly outside."

Puzzled, Sadie slipped on the coat and her warmest boots. "Where are we going?"

"We're taking a little trip down memory lane."

Before Sadie could question her further, she'd stepped outside where a sleigh with eight reindeer waited beside the front porch, Nick holding the reins.

Jody waved her into the back, and as soon as Sadie was seated, tucked a blanket around her. "The wind is brisk tonight," she explained, then climbed into the sleigh and handed her a cup of cocoa.

Nick flicked the reins and the reindeer shot forward, lifting into the sky. The air rushed over Sadie as the stars whizzed past overhead.

A sleigh ride with Jody and Nick—obviously her subconscious had turned them into the real Santa and Mrs. Claus. "Are we delivering Christmas presents?"

Nick's laugh bellowed over her. "It's still over a week until Christmas."

Talk about an accurate dream right down to the day. "Then what are we doing out here?"

Jody's smile lit up the dark sky. "I told you, we're taking a trip down memory lane."

What did that mean?

"Cookie?" Jody held out a plate of frosted Christmas cookies.

Sadie took one and settled back to eat it while she sipped her cocoa since knowing Jody and Nick as she did, they would explain when they were good and ready, and not a moment sooner.

Ten minutes later, they landed in the front yard of her childhood home. Jody jumped from the sleigh, and pushed the seat forward, but before Sadie could move a swirl of light filled the sky, a near match to the northern lights she and Hank had seen cross-country skiing.

Seconds later, the neon green and blue lights vanished, and Sadie sucked in a startled gasp when her mother's smiling face appeared along with Sadie's ten-year-old self.

"It's crooked." Her mom pointed to the lights her dad had just strung across the front porch.

A frown marring his normally, cheerful face, he said, "It's fine."

Her mother winked at her. "It's drooping."

He released a pent-up sigh, then reached over and straightened the lights. "Better?" he groused.

Sadie giggled and whispered in her mother's ear, her tinkling laughter filling the air.

"You're right, he is acting a lot like the Grinch," her mom said, in a loud stage whisper.

"What are my two best girls whispering about," he demanded, humor lacing his voice.

More giggles erupted. "Nothing," they echoed in unison.

Tears rushed to Sadie's eyes. She reached for her dad, but her hand went through him.

Jody tugged on her arm, but she resisted, not wanting to leave her parents.

The light descended again, and they were back in the sleigh. Moments later, they lifted off into the night sky.

"Why couldn't we stay?" The void that had filled her since her parents died returned as fresh and painful as all those years ago when she'd learned about the accident.

Jody twisted around to face her. "We have other places to be tonight."

Sadie stared at the cluster of stars shining down and wondered if her parents were up there watching over her. Were they proud of the woman she'd become? What would her life have been like if they'd lived?

She'd barely processed those thoughts when the sleigh landed next to her house. The lights appeared again, and she and Jody stood on the porch beside her and Hank.

"I love you, Sadie." Hank's voice floated over her, sending a shiver of awareness through her.

How she'd longed to hear those words. Her other self stepped away from him. "It's too soon. I won't rush into another marriage."

Hank's expression darkened. "Do you have feelings for me?"

She blanched. "You know I do."

"Then what are you waiting for?"

She silently stared up at him.

He squeezed her hands. "I'm not trying to pressure you, but I need to know if someday you'll return my feelings."

"I care about you Hank, and I think it might be love, but I need to be sure."

He smiled tenderly at her, hugging her close.

How many times had she said those exact words to him? What would she do if Hank grew tired of waiting?

A shiver swept over her as the lights appeared. Back in the sleigh, they jetted off a third time and returned to the farm, snow falling silently from the sky. An older Sadie with a sprinkling of gray in her hair stood at the entrance to the barn, a cat in her arms.

The quiet unsettled her. Where was everyone?

Jody said nothing. She just stood beside her.

"Why did you bring me here?"

Jody turned and squeezed her hands between hers. "This is future you."

Sadie swallowed back the fear clogging her throat and asked, "Where's Hank?"

Sympathy filled Jody's eyes. "He found someone else."

Sadie's heart seized. No Hank? "Did I meet someone else?"

"Yes, but none of them compared to Hank, so you chose to be alone."

Sadie stared at her older self, the loneliness etched in her face. Was this her future?

Jody's voice whispered over her. "The future is what you make it."

Before she could ask Jody to explain, the lights appeared. When she opened her eyes, she was alone in her bathtub, the water tepid. She climbed out and wrapped in a fluffy white towel, staring into the bathroom mirror. A dream. That's all it was, but it had felt so real.

She dismissed it as whimsical nonsense. Still, it was entirely possible she could end up like her future self in the vision. Is that what she wanted?

THE NEXT MORNING, Sadie dressed and went straight to the deli. Still shaken from her dream the night before, she asked Jody about it, but the older woman only gave her a blank stare. "Sleigh ride? What are you talking about?"

Sadie watched her closely for any sign of evasion, but found nothing. Finally, she smiled and with a wave of her hand said, "Must have been a dream."

Jody studied her a long moment, then said, "Dreams can feel very real."

Was that a twinkle she'd seen in Jody's eyes?

Before she could question her further, Jody waved and went down the hall to her waiting class.

Sadie watched until she disappeared, then went upstairs to her office and called Congresswoman Menudo before customers started arriving. Her secretary answered on the second ring.

Sadie identified herself and asked to speak with the congresswoman.

"I'm sorry. She's in Washington this week. Would you like the number for that office?"

"Yes, thank you."

Sadie hung up and dialed the DC number. Three rings later, she was connected with the congresswoman's secretary. "I'd like to speak with Congresswoman Menudo, please. This is Sadie McCluskey."

"Can I tell her what it's regarding?"

"Yes, we had a meeting a few weeks ago about funding and some other grants for my farm. I'm following up on that conversation."

"Wait, are you *the* Sadie McCluskey who runs McCluskey River Farm in Snowside?"

"Yes, are you from Vermont?" Sadie thought she'd detected a southern drawl, but she couldn't be sure.

"Oh no. I'm from Louisiana—born and bred. I know about your farm because the congresswoman has had me searching for funding for you."

Excitement built inside Sadie. "You have?"

"Yes ma'am. It's been a top priority for her."

Sadie's excitement switched to elation. "Does this mean you've found something?"

"Not yet, but I'm looking into several sources I think are really promising, and I hope to have some answers in the next few days that I'll pass on to the congresswoman."

"If the congresswomen has time, I'd like to speak to her."

"She's in session right now, but I think she might be available this afternoon. Would you have time, then?"

"I will. She can contact me on my cell." Sadie rattled off the number, said goodbye and hung up the phone. Maybe Elroy was right. Maybe she'd be able to get the funding after all.

CHAPTER 38

Hank headed north on Friday morning. He'd contacted Lydia and arranged to meet with her in a town that was about the halfway between Snowside and Angel Falls.

The more he'd thought about it, the more he'd agreed with his mom. He needed to talk to Lydia. He'd only seen her twice—when he'd told it was over and not to contact him or his family again, and at the mini mart at Thanksgiving. The first time he'd been so furious he could barely speak. This time his emotions were in check, and he was ready to face her.

He arrived at the coffeehouse and found a corner table away from prying eyes. Hank ordered a coffee, more for something to put his hands around than for any real need for a drink.

Lydia showed up fifteen minutes later and sat across from him. She arched a brow, her gaze censuring. "You didn't order me a coffee?"

Hank shrugged. "It would've been cold."

She gave a delicate snort. "Is this about me being late?"

He met her exasperated gaze dead on. "No, it's not. I'm not here to pick a fight. You were the one who asked to meet." His fingers tightened around the cup, his pulse thudding as he contained his irritation. "What do you want?"

Lydia's harsh expression eased. "Let me get my coffee before we get into this."

Hank studied the dingy coffee shop as he waited for her to return.

Minutes later, she claimed her seat and added diet sweetener to her coffee. She took out a napkin, set the stir stick on it, and inhaled deeply before looking up at him. "I'm surprised you finally agreed to meet me."

The anger that had simmered inside him since he'd discovered Lydia's deception, rose again. "You tried to swindle my mom. That's not something I'm likely to forget or forgive."

Lydia had the grace to look ashamed. "I'll admit it's not something I'm proud of, but it was a good deal."

Hank stared at her in disbelief. "For you, especially when you've got an inspector in your pocket willing to lie about what's wrong with the property and drive the price down so you could buy it for a fraction of what it's worth."

She stirred her coffee, watching him. "Your mom still would have made a lot of money."

"But not nearly as much as what she could get if you hadn't lied. And money isn't everything. That pub has been in my family since the turn of the twentieth century. Mom would never have considered selling if you hadn't pressed her. Some things are more precious than money."

She hitched a shoulder. "I've never been particularly sentimental." She sipped her coffee as if to bolster herself, then met his gaze. "I never meant to hurt you. I'm sorry."

Hank silently absorbed the information. He blew out a weary breath, studying her face—the deep-set eyes, perfect nose, and rosebud mouth. Once upon a time, he couldn't keep his eyes off her, but no more. When a face came to mind these days, he saw soft brown hair, sparkling green eyes, and full lips he couldn't wait to kiss.

"Is it serious with the woman I saw you with?"

Hank considered her question. "Is that why you asked me here? To pump me for information?"

She shrugged. "You've answered my question for me. I'm glad you found someone. I'd really like it if we could stop being enemies."

Hank studied the woman he'd been certain he'd spend his life with. Those feelings were gone—if they'd really been there at all. "I get the sense you had another reason for contacting me."

Her teeth sunk into her lower lip. "I'm leaving Angel Falls."

"You could have texted that."

She nodded. "I could have, but I need a favor."

This made more sense. "What?"

Her fingers tensed around the coffee cup. "I'm applying for a job in Boston. I need a letter from you."

"Saying what exactly?"

"That I've learned my lesson, I've tried to mend my ways, and that you're willing to give me a second chance."

Hank rocked back in his chair. "Seriously?"

A dull red swept over her cheeks. "I know I'm asking a lot after what I did, but I haven't been able to get a job since you filed that ethics complaint with the Board of Realtors. I need to make a fresh start, and if you could do this for me, I know I could get the job." She paused, her gaze turned pleading. "I really need that fresh start."

"How do I know you won't swindle someone else?"

"You don't, but I swear I won't." A flicker of vulnerability passed over her eyes, her hands squeezing together. "Please, will you help me?"

He wanted to refuse, but he hesitated. What if forgiveness

stopped the fury burning in his gut? "Okay, text me the information and I'll write it for you."

"Really?" She squeezed his hand. "Thank you."

Hank studied her, trying to determine her sincerity. "I believe in second chances, so this is yours. I'll be checking with your employer, and if I suspect you're up to your old tricks, my last complaint will look like a thank-you note in comparison to what I'll write next."

"You won't regret it."

Hank hoped she told him the truth. He told her goodbye, then got into his truck and headed home. As he took the interstate back to Snowside, the knot in his gut eased, and it occurred to him that he'd gotten the closure he hadn't even known he'd needed.

SADIE FINISHED SETTING up the Pin the Nose on Rudolph booth Saturday morning. She couldn't believe Christmas was just a week away.

Jody came up to the booth, carrying an enormous platter of cookies that they'd baked the day before. Christmas carols had played as they'd made batch after batch of cookies, some frosted, some not, for the cookie frosting booth. Much to Sadie's surprise, she hadn't minded the music. In fact, she'd seen less and less of her inner Grinch rearing its head. Nick and Jody had even done a little dance. A perfect day, except Hank hadn't been there. He'd told her he had an appointment and couldn't make it with no explanation. Was he hiding something?

The dream came back to haunt her. Would she end up alone?

Pushing the thoughts from her mind, she focused on the carnival. In just a few hours, they opened the first—and hopefully many more to come—Christmas on Ice carnival to the public.

Sadie moved from booth to booth, admiring Jody's vision

brought to life. She could never have done this without her and Nick, not to mention Elroy, Mickey, Jack, and Annie. They'd all pitched in to help with the carnival.

"What do you think?" Jody asked, waving the platter under her nose.

"I think they look just like they did last night—good enough to eat." Sadie selected a cookie from the tray and took a bite, then rubbed her belly. "They taste as good as they look."

Jody's delighted laughter woke Prancer curled up next to Sweet Pea. "I'm glad to hear it."

"What's next on the list?" Sadie asked.

Jody rattled off all the things that still needed to be done, and Sadie had her doubts they'd accomplish it all before they opened. "We're going to need ten more people to open on time."

"That's why I have reinforcements lined up."

"Who?"

Jody set the cookies down and gestured across the room at Nick, who stood with Elroy and half a dozen brawny men Sadie had never seen before. How did Jody always have volunteers at her beck and call?

HANK ARRIVED at the farm at nine. He desperately wanted to talk to Sadie alone, but he knew there wouldn't be time until tonight. Instead, he went to help set up the carnival.

Jody immediately put him to work on the Fish for a Present Booth.

Nick came up beside him. "Looking good."

"Thanks, but I'm not sure we've got enough presents."

Nick slapped a hand on Hank's shoulder and squeezed. "No worries. I'm sure I've got more in my bag." He rummaged through the enormous red bag he'd had over his shoulder and pulled out several wrapped gifts, handing them to Hank.

"Now that we've got that set, Jody's in the back with your costume."

Hank hadn't been much of a costume guy until he'd started teaching kindergartners. He'd quickly learned his kids loved to dress up, especially when their teacher did.

He found Jody in Sadie's office with Sadie dressed in a red velvet tunic with white trim and black tights that hugged all her sweet curves he longed to run his hands over. His thoughts focused on taking her in his arms and kissing her until her cheeks turned as bright as her tunic.

Jody thrust a costume at him. "Here's yours."

Hank looked it over, on board with everything but the tights. There was no way he could squeeze into them. He handed them back to Jody. "I'll do everything but the tights."

Jody's eyes took on a hard glint. "Kings wore tights back in the day."

Hank gestured to Sadie's outfit. "Queens didn't. How about I'll be a modern day king versus a medieval one?"

Jody frowned and looked ready to object when Sadie broke in. "I think that's a fine idea."

Hank mouthed, "Thank you," grateful for her support. "Where do I change?" he asked, before Jody could raise another objection.

CHAPTER 39

As per Jody's instructions, Hank and Sadie greeted people at the entrance to the carnival. The kiddos were hopped up as if they'd been injected with an IV shot full of caffeine, giggling, jumping, and darting from booth to booth, their parents trying unsuccessfully to corral them.

A line formed where Nick sat in the massive red chair as children waited impatiently to tell him what they wanted for Christmas.

Sadie whispered to Hank. "Looks like the carnival is a huge success. Not a surprise, with Jody and Nick at the helm."

Hank nodded his agreement. "No question about it. Those two know how to put together an event."

Minutes later, Jody darted past, checking booths to make sure they had enough supplies. She moved Sadie and Hank from greeting people to Pin the Tail on Rudolph and Fish for a Present booths, then scurried off.

Sadie's booth had a continual line of kids and parents over the next two hours. She looked up to find Congresswoman Menudo at her booth. What was she doing here?

"Sadie, it's so good to see you again." She waved a hand over the carnival. "This is such a marvelous idea, and I love the booths. You've done a fabulous job."

Sadie couldn't take credit. "I agree. It looks great, but it wasn't me. My volunteer is the brains behind this."

"Well, she's done an incredible job, but I find it impossible to believe your vision isn't part of this." She winked at Sadie. "Every time I come here, you just keep making improvements. It's amazing."

Pleasure sizzled through her. "I have more ideas than time or money." She started to ask about the status of her loan when Kirstin and Henry came up.

"Where is the Fishing for Presents booth?" Kirstin asked, her eyes bright with anticipation.

Sadie pointed to Hank's booth next to her.

Kirstin bounced in her wheelchair as Henry pushed her to the booth. Sadie watched the kids interact with Hank a moment then turned back to Sheila, only to find she'd disappeared into the crowd.

Disappointment filled her, but she shoved it aside as more kids arrived at her booth.

An hour later, Jody stood beside Nick and rang a bell to gather everyone around. When the crowd went silent, Jody said, "Thank you all for coming to our first annual Christmas on Ice. I have a bit of news to share. Nicky and I are going home after the holidays, but we didn't want to leave Sadie or Hank high and dry. Unbeknownst to them, I took on the job search and found the perfect replacements for us."

Jody gestured to a woman dressed as an elf, and Sadie gasped when she recognized Hank's mother. "Sally Dabrowski has agreed to fill in for me—indefinitely."

"What? You live in Angel Falls. How would this work?" Sadie asked, crossing over to them.

"I do," Hank's mother said, a wide smile crossing her face.

"But Elroy convinced me that since I'm retiring I might want to try something new, and this would be a great place to do so. And since we don't get to see each other that often, he invited me to stay with him, providing me with the perfect opportunity to spend time with him and try my hand at event planning. That is, if you'll have me?"

Momentarily speechless, Sadie pulled herself together. "I definitely want you, and I can't think of anyone better suited for the job than you. My only concern is that I'd be cutting into your time with Elroy."

Elroy stood next to Nick, and piped up, "The fact is, we're both going to be busy because I'll be spending three days a week taking over for Nick in Hank's classroom." His gaze shot to his great-nephew. "That is, if you'll have me?"

Hank came to stand beside Sadie, and looked equally speechless. "Of course. You're the perfect replacement."

Jody clapped her hands. "Excellent. Now that we have that settled, I want to introduce Sheila Menudo, our local representative. She's asked for a moment of your time."

Sadie's radar went up when Sheila moved next to Jody. "Sadie McCluskey and I met a few weeks ago when she came to my office in need of my assistance to buy her farm. She told me about the plans she has for it. Already an amazing operation, her vision for the future is incredible. I'm so pleased to be a part of bringing her dreams together, which will benefit the entire city."

She turned to Sadie. "My aides worked late into the night, and we finally received notice that your loan has been approved. This is monumental, not only because there are so few women in agriculture, but also urban farms in general are overlooked. They are such an important part of our city. We don't want to lose them." Sheila held out her hand to Sadie.

Overcome with emotion, Sadie had to swallow twice before

she could utter a sound. "Thank you. I can't tell you how much this means to me. I couldn't have done it without you."

Sheila waved off her gratitude. "Nonsense. With your determination, you would have been successful with or without me. I'm just grateful my staff and I could facilitate it sooner rather than later." She paused, then continued. "But there's more. Sadie shared with me that her dreams went beyond purchasing the farm to also acquiring the adjacent property to build generational housing for families centered around the farm and a community garden. My staff applied for grants for this project, along with the loan, and they've also been approved."

Sheila lifted a cloth covering a table that Sadie hadn't noticed before. "Elroy Dabrowski, a retired architect and current owner of the property Sadie farms, designed this model including the potential for purchasing the adjacent property, which I'm sure will change with Sadie's input, since this is all a surprise to her."

Sadie's jaw dropped. She crossed to the table, staring at Elroy's creation, exactly as she'd described it to him. Her mentor and friend appeared at her elbow. "I told you to have faith and it would happen, didn't I?"

Sadie gazed at him, so moved by what he'd done, she couldn't find the words to express her gratitude. "I can't believe you did this. Is this the project you've been working on?"

He nodded.

Taking comfort in Elroy's presence, she leaned her head against his shoulder.

"I'm so happy your dreams are coming true," Elroy said. "You've worked hard, and you deserve it. You've accomplished something few women have been able to do, and you're making inroads for young girls everywhere."

"Thank you for having faith in me and for helping me bring this all together." She raised her voice for the group to hear. "This is beyond anything I could've imagined and exactly what I dreamed of."

Her gaze cut to Hank. Would he be here to share it with her or would she drive him away?

Jody's words echoed in her head.

The future is what you make it.

Elroy pressed a kiss to her cheek, then winked at her, and said, "I think you may have a few more surprises in store."

"What are you talking about?" Sadie asked.

"You'll find out soon enough," he said, then disappeared into the crowd before she could press him for answers.

People crowded around the table congratulating her. Before she could take it all in, Hank materialized at her elbow with a man who looked vaguely familiar. They moved over to stand beside Jody. "There's one more announcement I'd like to share," Hank said. "While Ms. Menudo pulled the funding together, I did a little nosing around and spoke to a contractor about building the housing on the adjacent property. I'm sure Tim needs no introduction from me as most of you are familiar with his reality show, *Paying It Back*. He's agreed to build the housing project on Sadie's site. I'm going to let him explain what happens next."

Hank stepped back, and Tim spoke to the crowd as Sadie could only stare. Hank had put her dream into motion to become reality, and what had she done for him? Refused to open her heart, that's what.

"I'm so pleased to be here today and eager to start this project," Tim said. "Not only is this helping Sadie, but it will also bring affordable housing to our city." He turned to Sadie. "That is, of course, assuming Sadie is on board with it."

All eyes turned to Sadie who could only gulp air. Finally, she pulled herself together, and smiling said, "How can I say no to such a generous offer? Thank you so much. With your help I know it will be amazing."

A round of applause went through the crowd. Sadie felt like the luckiest woman alive. Before she could thank Hank, he moved off-stage. She scanned the crowd, but saw no sign of him. Where had he gone?

Sheila came up to her. "I hope you don't mind that I sprung all of this on you here instead of announcing it in private," she said. "Rather than return your call, I came to the farm and you were out. Jody asked me why I was here, and when I told her, she insisted I save the announcement for today. She said she couldn't think of a better place to celebrate."

Jody was right. This was the perfect time to reveal it. "The woman is never wrong."

"She's a force of nature," Sheila agreed.

"That is the perfect way to describe her."

"There are more details about the loan I'll share with you later. You're set to sign papers the day after Christmas."

Sadie sucked in a surprised breath. "How is that possible? Loans never go through that fast, especially government loans."

Sheila offered her a sly smile. "I called in all my favors on this one. There was no way I was going to let it drag out any longer, but I have a favor to ask."

"Anything."

"After you sign the papers, I'd like to set up a photo shoot. It would mean so much to other women and small farmers to know that this is an achievable goal."

"I'd be happy to."

She and Sheila hugged, then she left, telling her one of her aides would be in touch.

The sun shone down from the dazzling blue sky onto the property that would soon belong to her. All of her dreams were coming true. If only she had someone to share it with.

Sadie searched the crowd for Hank and found him with several kids at the snow angel booth. She smiled, watching as he laid in the snow with them making snow angels. By getting McGriff on board to build the housing project, he'd launched her dream into reality. Her heart fluttered when she realized he checked off all the boxes she wanted in a man.

CHAPTER 40

Three days to Christmas

Sadie's phone dinged with a text on Thursday morning. She glanced at it. Her vision blurred as she read Hank's invitation for her and Sweet Pea to spend Christmas Eve with him. She wanted it so badly, then remembered her dream. What if she'd been alone because she'd been too clingy and drove him away like she did with Luke?

Jody stood at her elbow, making bows for a variety of gifts. The woman was a serious savant at bow making and had a waiting list for her class. Fortunately, Sally rivaled Jody's skills at bow making, and crafts in general.

Sally had gone home yesterday to spend the holidays with her family, promising to return after Christmas.

"What do you think?" Jody asked. Sadie blinked, then looked at her latest creation with more than a touch of envy. "It's stunning. I don't know how you do it."

"It's easy. I can teach you."

Sadie shook her head. "I think I'm missing the bow-making gene."

"Nonsense, anyone can learn."

Sadie's phone dinged, reminding her she hadn't responded to Hank's text.

Jody arched a brow. "Don't you think you should answer that?"

She should, but she didn't want to.

"Yes, I'll answer it in a minute."

Jody stood beside her unmoving.

Sighing, Sadie answered the text.

Aren't you going to Angel Falls for Christmas?

He responded instantly.

Staying in Snowside to celebrate the holiday with my best girls.

Why don't we meet tonight so you can go to Angel Falls to celebrate Christmas Eve with your family?

Three dots appeared, then, *I'm staying here and can't meet tonight.*

He wasn't making this easy. She hadn't celebrated Christmas since her divorce, and the idea of doing so scared her.

Worse than being alone the rest of your life?

Valid point.

What time?

I'll be by tomorrow to help until closing, then we'll go to my place.

Why don't we just order pizza and stay here?

Better to be on her own turf.

A pause, then Hank sent a thumbs-up emoji.

Sadie tucked the phone into her pocket as she realized she'd be celebrating Christmas for the first time in almost a decade.

JODY, Nick, and Elroy met after Sadie went home for the day.

"We have a problem." Jody said, before the men settled into their seats.

Elroy's bushy brows rose to a point high on his forehead. "What? So far as I can tell, everything is going as planned. Sadie got the funding so she can buy the farm, McGriff is going to build the houses, and Hank's in love with her. And I'm certain she's in love with him. What could possibly be wrong?"

"I don't disagree with any of those points, but I'm telling you, something's up. I can feel it in here." She pressed a hand over her chest. "Sadie hasn't told Hank everything about her past."

"So if your Ghosts of Christmas Past didn't convince her to do that, what do we do now?" Elroy asked.

Nick gave him a subtle shake of his head, but too late to stop Jody from demanding, "Are you suggesting I've failed? After all the years we've known each other, have you forgotten about my sixth sense when it comes to love?"

Elroy cast a glance at Nick, who rolled his eyes as if to say, what were you thinking?

"I'm sorry. You, better than anyone, knows matchmaking. I've known that since you set me up with Myra."

Jody's frown eased, and she gave a nod of approval. "That's better. Now let's talk about how we can ensure that these two get their happily-ever-after by Christmas and for every Christmas after."

Nick steepled his fingers together. "What can we do to help?"

Jody smiled and nodded. "That's more like it. I know Christmas Eve is extremely busy for you, but if you and Elroy could facilitate getting Hank's surprise for Sadie together that would be a huge help. I've got a Christmas gift for Hank in mind that will be the perfect gift from Sadie and that should bring everything together."

"We can definitely do that." Nick glanced at Elroy who nodded his agreement.

"That's going to entail getting her house decorated with a tree and all the trimmings because we're not only bringing her together with Hank, but we have to make her believe in Christmas and all the magic that comes with it."

"I have an idea that would help Hank give Sadie a memorable Christmas," Elroy said.

Jody eyed him. "What have you got in mind?"

"Well, I was thinking that if I invited Sally to bring the family to Snowside for Christmas, then Sadie would have that big family Christmas she's always wanted."

Jody tapped a finger against her chin. "That's a splendid idea."

"I'll call Sally tonight and get it arranged, then we can surprise Hank and Sadie Christmas morning."

"Excellent. We have a plan in place. Let's get these two love-birds together for the holidays." Prancer popped up his head from Jody's lap and barked his approval.

CHAPTER 41

Christmas Eve

Sadie threw back the covers and rolled out of bed Christmas Eve morning, even though it was still pitch black outside. Pulling on her clothes, she went downstairs to start the coffee. When it finished brewing, she poured it into a travel mug, bundled up, and headed to the barn to feed the animals, Sweet Pea trotting alongside her. When she finished her chores, she went to the deli, which was where Jody found her.

"I didn't expect to see you here. I thought you'd be out doing chores."

"All done," Sadie said. "What's on tap today?"

Jody studied her closely, and Sadie fought the urge to squirm beneath her scrutiny.

But much to her surprise, Jody didn't comment. Instead, she said, "Stocking the shelves for last-minute gifts, and hopefully we have enough preserves and arts and crafts on hand."

"If we sell out, everyone goes home early."

Jody nodded in agreement, then set to work helping Sadie get ready for the lunch crowd. When they finished, Sadie ran up to her office to put the finishing touches on Hank's Christmas gift. She'd struggled to think of something that had just the right meaning and this had come to her last night. She signed the card and tucked it into the envelope, then slipped it into her pocket and went downstairs just in time to open the store.

Sadie stayed so busy, she missed Hank's arrival and didn't see him until sometime after lunch when she spotted him outside with Sweet Pea. Her heart beat a little faster. He was here and spending Christmas Eve with her. She fingered the envelope in her pocket and wondered what his reaction would be. Would it bring them closer or drive a wedge between them?

Jody called for more jam from the storage room. When she returned, Hank was gone.

By three o'clock, most of the customers had dwindled away, and Sadie decided to send everyone home.

She hugged Jody and Nick, her heart heavy as she knew this was goodbye. Elroy on their heels. Dale hugged her and promised to see her bright and early Monday morning when they reopened the farm.

Now, she was alone with Hank, but he was nowhere to be seen. Had he left? Was the dream coming true before she had a chance to make it right with Hank?

Her heart shriveled at the thought just like the Grinch's.

She shut off the lights, tugged on her coat, then whistled for Sweet Pea, but she didn't come running. Sadie went outside and whistled again.

No sign of the dog.

Assuming she'd gone to the house to wait on the porch, Sadie made her way home, her heart heavy. As she drew near the house, she heard the faint strains of Christmas music, but it did nothing to lighten her mood any more than the dark, gloomy sky overhead. The only light came from the single porch light. Inside, the house was dark and empty just like her heart. She'd waited too long, and Hank had given up on her. The envelope in her pocket suddenly felt like a lead weight.

She climbed the steps, reached for the doorknob, then froze when she noticed the massive wreath on the door. Where had that come from? Christmas lights strung over the porch rail flashed on as the knob twisted underneath her fingers. Sweet Pea rushed out, tail wagging as she danced around her legs.

"How did you get inside?"

Sweet Pea barked once, then plopped down on the porch, staring up at her. Sadie raised her eyes to find Hank in the doorway. Her heart fluttered, and she offered him a tentative smile. "What are you doing here?"

Hank ushered them both inside and closed the door, taking her coat from her. "What do you mean? We made plans to spend Christmas together."

"Well, yes, but when I didn't see you, I assumed—"

Hank started at her in disbelief. "You thought I'd walk out on you on Christmas Eve and not tell you I was leaving. What kind of man do you think I am?" He folded her into his arms and hugged her tight. "I'm Hank, not Luke, and I'm going to keep telling you that until you believe it."

Sadie gulped as the Whos in Whoville started singing. She slipped out of his arms and moved to the fireplace, then froze when she saw the massive Christmas tree beside the sofa fully decorated with gifts piled underneath. Her gaze circled the cozy living room. Garland looped over the mantel, and a side table held a tiny Christmas village that was a replica of her farm. Music played softly in the background. Who had done all this?

Her gaze moved to Hank. "Did you decorate the house?"

"I did, with a lot of direction from Nick and Elroy."

She fingered a cherished childhood ornament—a picture-framed bell with a photo of her and her parents. "Where did you find this?" she whispered, gazing up at Hank.

"I don't know. Jody, I assume." Hank silently studied her. "You don't look happy." He stepped closer, the rough timbre of his voice vibrating through her. "Is this a problem?"

Her eyes filled with tears, and she rapidly blinked them back. It was beautiful and reminded her of the decorations she'd put up with such care all those years ago when she'd had so much hope and expectation.

Tiny farm animals and glittery balls in purple, pink, and silver ornaments hung from the tree and sparkled in the low light. "No, it's lovely. Thank you for doing this."

A slow melody came over the speakers, and Hank slid his arms around her. They glided around the room.

Hank twirled her in a circle as the song played and the lyrics spoke to her.

If you've got a dream, grab it. If you love him, don't let go.

Their bodies fused together, his breath warm against her ear as he murmured, "I love you, Sadie."

If you love him, never let him go.

When the song ended, Hank guided her over to the sofa, and they sat down, their knees touching. Before she lost her nerve, she reached into her pocket and held out the envelope to him. Her hand trembled as he took it from her.

"What's this?"

"An early Christmas present."

Sweet Pea, head on paws, stared at them.

Sadie watched as Hank took the card from the envelope. A couple danced on the outside with *dance of a lifetime* written underneath them. Her breath caught as he read her carefully crafted words.

Hank,

You've asked me about Luke, and I've stalled telling you about this time of my life, but you deserve to hear it all. I decided to go old school and write it down.

Luke asked me to marry him three months after we met, and I said yes. We were married two weeks later, a small civil ceremony in early June.

We were both working long hours, and the summer flew past. Fall arrived and I couldn't wait for our first Christmas together. Right after Thanksgiving, I pestered him until we bought a tree. I decorated it, baked cookies and pies, shopped for the perfect present for Luke, his parents, his siblings.

The more excited I got about the holidays, the more distant he became, and I attributed it to the long hours he'd been working. A week before Christmas I stopped by his office with dinner. He wasn't there, so I went to his lab and found him making out with his grad student. I rushed out, but he caught up to me. He told me it was all too much—the marriage, the holidays. He needed space and said it was all my fault because I was too needy.

Hank's gaze cut to her, and Sadie's heart thudded in her ears as their eyes locked and held, then he went back to reading.

He carried his burden of guilt for sure, and I certainly don't excuse his infidelity—infidelities I found out later—but I'd been desperately lonely when I met him, and I used him to fill my emptiness.

A week after Christmas, divorce papers arrived, and two months later, we were divorced. I signed a lease with Elroy the next day, and I swore I'd never rush into a relationship again or be hurt like that again.

I love you, Hank, with every fiber of my being. You are the only man for me. You're everything I've ever wanted, and the one person I can tell anything. I swear I'll always be as open with you as you've been with me.

Love,

Sadie.

He looked at her, and Sadie's heart constricted as she waited for his response. "Thank you for this gift. It's perfect, and for the record, Luke was a jerk and never deserved your love. You are perfect just as you are. I love you, Sadie McCluskey." He signaled Sweet Pea, and she obediently trotted over and sat down in front of Sadie, a big red bow tied around her neck.

Hank gestured to the dog. "We have an early present for you, too."

Sadie arched a brow. "You're giving me Sweet Pea?"

Hank grinned, shaking his head. "No, she's playing postman tonight, or more accurately postdog."

Hank got down on his knee and removed the bag tied to her collar. He took out a black velvet box and opened it, a glittering engagement ring tucked inside.

"Sadie McCluskey, will you marry me?"

Sadie sucked in a breath, her whole body trembling.

The Whos in Whoville broke into song again, their voices so loud, the music so beautiful, that Sadie didn't bother to shush them. Her Grinch's heart grew ten times bigger than her own.

Her gaze locked with Hank's, and she smiled through her tears as she pushed her fears aside. "Yes, yes, yes, I will marry you."

Hank slid the ring on her finger, then rose, lifting her to her feet. He kissed her, a kiss so tender and soft, her heart nearly burst with love. She threw her arms around him and deepened the kiss, putting all the pent-up emotion inside her into it. When she pulled back, she whispered, "I love you."

He traced his fingers across her cheek, his eyes dark with passion. "I love you, too, more than I've ever loved anyone."

She finally had the man of her dreams, and Christmas with a man who would always be there for her.

EPILOGUE

Hank drove Sadie and Sweet Pea to Elroy's Christmas morning to spend the day with him, and to share their news about their Christmas engagement. The snow continued to fall, leaving everything pristine and white.

He parked in front of Elroy's, and Sweet Pea in her excitement, leapt over the back seat and out Sadie's door the instant she stepped out of the truck. She loped through the snow and up the porch, the Christmas bells on her collar announcing her arrival as she skidded to a halt at the door, giving a loud bark.

Elroy swung open the door, and Sweet Pea vaulted inside.

"It's about time you two got here. I was beginning to wonder if you'd forgotten."

"When have you ever heard of me missing out on a Christmas meal?" Hank asked.

Elroy chuckled and ushered them inside, their arms loaded with gifts. His brows arched. "I told you, you didn't need to bring gifts," he groused. "Since you did, you might as well put them under the tree." Beneath the gruffness, Hank saw delight on his face.

Sadie put the presents underneath the massive tree, and a dozen or more voices shouted "Merry Christmas".

She turned to find Hank's entire family, including Annie, Jack, Zoe, and Tony, rush in from the kitchen, sweeping her and Hank into their embrace, his mother leading the charge.

"What are you doing here?" Hank asked. "I thought you were staying in Angel Falls until after the holidays?"

"That's what I'd intended until Elroy invited all of us here to celebrate Christmas, and we thought it would be a nice change of pace, so we came." Sally took Sadie into her arms and hugged her close, then looked down at her finger. Beaming at her son, she said, "So, you took my advice and asked her."

"I did," Hank said.

Sadie's heart expanded with love when Sally pulled them into a group hug. "I'm so happy." She squeezed Sadie's hands. "Welcome to the family."

Sadie's eyes met Hank's. He'd given her the perfect Christmas —one she'd always cherish. And the icing on the cake, Hank came with a readymade family.

Nick started the Mini Cooper, tired but content after a long, busy season. "You did it again."

Jody gazed up at Nick. "*We* did." She dabbed her eyes with a tissue. "I just love a happy ending, don't you?"

Nick shifted into gear and pressed down on the accelerator, startling a laugh from her and a bark from Prancer. "I most certainly do, but the best happy ending I've ever had is with you."

The blue of Jody's eyes deepened. "Oh, Nicky, you always say just the right thing."She leaned over and pressed a kiss to his cheek. "Let's go home."

"Ho, ho, ho and a Merry Christmas," Nick bellowed, as they headed north to prepare for the next Christmas romance.

The end.

Preview
Book one, Santa Comes to Snowside
A Sweet Christmas Romance

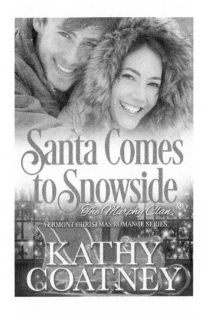

Snowside, Vermont
N*ovember*

"WELL, Nicky, where are we off to this Christmas holiday?"

Nicholas Claws arched bushy brows as he glanced at his wife, Jody, seated beside him in their candy cane red Mini Cooper convertible. He shifted into high gear and punched the gas just enough to throw her head back. The wind tossed her silver curls, producing the tinkling laugh he loved.

"One of our worker bees found a place I think you'll love. It's a nonprofit called Job Hunters 4 You, and Jack Davidson, the man who started it has the kind of giving nature that's right up your alley. He helps the low income and unemployed find work by providing them with work clothes, help writing résumés, and even has a hair salon onsite."

Jody's smile warmed him through and through. "I love it! Tell me more."

"Well, our visionary, Mr. Davidson, saw a need in the community, gave up a lucrative career and swanky high-rise apartment on the upper eastside of Snowside, invested his savings and retirement to buy a rundown warehouse in the industrial section. He's currently living above it to save money."

Jody's blue eyes rounded beneath wire-rimmed glasses. "And he's doing this all on his own?"

"Not totally. Mickey Roberts, his uncle, supported his vision from the start, and he manages the hair salon at Job Hunters 4 You. The downturn in the economy several years ago started Jack on his path to enlightenment. White collar workers were laid off, including his best friend who almost lost everything. Mickey struggled, too, after returning from Iraq, and if not for Jack he could have ended up on the street three Christmases ago."

Jody stroked Prancer, the miniature poodle asleep on her lap. "Well, color me intrigued. This sounds like a perfect holiday project for us, but will we be able to make it home in time to finish our Christmas village?"

"I know you're eager to get your miniature village setup, but we will get it done. It might be tight, but we've always been home for Christmas, and Job Hunters 4 You could definitely use some volunteer support to keep it running. I don't see how we can pass this up, do you?" He flipped the blinker to the left and pulled onto the freeway, heading south.

"No, we can't. This project is just what we've been looking for. We've got a nonprofit that needs a bit of help, and we can't walk away from that, but you haven't told me much about Jack."

Nick might have found the perfect nonprofit for them, but Jody always wanted to know about the people—in particular, their relationship status. "Jack's single, estranged from his parents, and at the moment unattached, but I think there's a prospect that with your special touch could bring about a holiday romance."

Jody lifted her face to the unseasonably warm sunshine, the bare trees marking the beginning of the holiday season.

"Then we not only need to work on the romance, but also bring Jack back together with his parents."

"There's also a teenager named Tony who needs our assistance. He's a non-believer."

"Oh my, we can't have that. We'll have to come up with a Christmas miracle or two to get him back on track."

"You read my mind."

"Oh, I do love the challenge of a new project. It's like the first flush of love. Do you remember when we first met?"

His wife looked over at him, rosy cheeks and blue eyes twinkling as bright as the silver bells dangling from her earlobes.

"How could I forget? You bring it up every year when we start a new project."

"So what attracted you to me? My cookies or hot chocolate?"

A loaded question that he wasn't about to debate again. There was only one correct answer. "Both."

Jody winked at him. "Good answer."

Nick pressed down on the accelerator and headed toward

Vermont where they would spend the duration of the Christmas holiday.two

Santa Comes to Snowside
Need more Christmas romance? Download the Crooked Halo Christmas Chronicles Box Set right now!

GET A FREE BOOK

Angels R' Us

Saving lost souls is hard work. Just ask Olivia and Zack, two angels who've been assigned to bring Maggie and Ian together. Zack was Olivia's CIA partner in life, and he's become her nemesis in death. What Olivia doesn't realize is that Zack has vowed to love her into eternity.

Subscribe to my newsletter to get your copy of Angels R' Us here.

https://kathycoatney.com/subscribe

ALSO BY KATHY COATNEY

Thank you for reading *Jingle all the Way to Snowside,* book 2 in *A Vermont Christmas Romance—The Murphy Clan series*.

If you liked this book, I'd love it if you'd leave a review at Goodreads and BookBub.

I love hearing from my fans. You can contact me through my website, newsletter, or join my Facebook group Kathy Coatney's The Beauty Bowl. I share information about my books, excerpts, and other fun information. If you like free books come join Kathy Coatney's Review Team by sending me an email kathy@kathycoatney.com.

All my books are small town, contemporary romances with uplifting stories of hope, a sprinkling of quirky characters and a happily ever after sure to leave you with a smile.

Contact me at:

Website

Kathy Coatney's The Beauty Bowl

The Murphy Clan

Falling in Love series

Falling For You…Again

Falling in Love With You

Falling in Love For The First Time

Falling in Love With Him

Return to Hope's Crossing series

Forever His

Forever Mine

Forever Yours

Crooked Halo Christmas Chronicles

Be My Santa Tonight

Her Christmas Wish

Under the Mistletoe

The Christmas Kiss—A Sweet Christmas Romance

A Vermont Christmas Romance

Santa Comes to Snowside

Jingle all the Way to Snowside

Box Sets

Falling in Love Box Set

Return to Hope's Crossing Box Set

The Murphy Clan Mixed Collection

Crooked Halo Christmas Chronicles Box Set

ABOUT THE AUTHOR

I've spent long hours behind the lens of a camera, wading through cow manure, rice paddies and orchards over my thirty-year career as a photojournalist specializing in agriculture.

I also love—and write—deeply emotional, small-town contemporary romance. Ironically, some of my books carry an agriculture thread in them, some more than others. Please note I used to write these books under Kate Curran, but now I write all books under Kathy Coatney.

I also writes a series of nonfiction children's books, From the Farm to the Table and Dad's Girls.

When I'm not writing, you'll find me mountain biking, cross-country skiing, or running—a really, really slow jog that's been compared to a pace slower than a tortoise.

Made in the USA
Coppell, TX
30 November 2022

87463526R00152